Unknown Assailant

By Lina Gardiner

I0457395

Copyright © 2014 Lina Gardiner

This book is a work of fiction. References to real people, establishments, organizations, or locations are intended only to provide a sense of authenticity, and are used fictitiously. The characters and events portrayed in this book are fictitious, and are not to be construed as real. Any similarity to real persons, living or dead, is coincidental and not intended by the authors.

Cover by Erin Dameron-Hill
Editor: Joyce Lamb
Beta Reader: Nola Richardson

Chapter One

Every night after work, Liz Davis parked her car in front of the two-story white house accented with black shutters and glistening red door. A lump formed in her throat. This picture-perfect exterior couldn't have been further from the truth. And now, to make everything worse, she'd gotten fired today.

Dry leaves leftover from last fall rustled on the lawn, making the skin tingle on the back of her neck. Thickening shadows near the shrubbery next to the garage door made her search for shapes that shouldn't be there. With the latest rash of vandalism, she'd been rattled. Luckily, the shadows were just shadows.

She opened the front door and relocked it the second she got inside. Her parents had died in a car accident a year ago and her world had gone haywire ever since. Maybe she was actually losing her mind because she'd swear someone was trying to deliberately scare her.

Her anxiety had cost her her job. Not that she'd ever fit in there. She'd been too preoccupied to do a half-decent job as a front store manager.

Two days ago the police department had closed the year-old file on her parents' deaths. The ruling stated the motor vehicle crash had been an accident.

She'd reminded the investigator about the acts of vandalism still happening to her. She'd personally phoned the police on several occasions for flat tires, broken windows, and other incidents.

She'd seen the same look in the officer's eyes that she'd seen in her co-workers' expressions. Everyone thought she was making it all up to keep her parents' file open.

She'd had no luck trying to contact her uncle since her parents had died and now she was alone. No friends, no family, and no one to turn to.

Going down the hallway into the kitchen, she made for the teakettle. A hot cup of tea would soothe her nerves. She let out a shaky breath and wondered what she'd do now. No job. The police didn't believe her, and she didn't feel safe in her own home.

She flicked the switch on the electric kettle—her hand barely touched the ceramic mug on the first shelf when the lights snapped out. She jumped and knocked a mug onto the granite counter top, where it shattered instantly. She heard and felt the tiny shards bouncing off the counter.

That thought left her quickly because silence buzzed the room like a three-alarm fire. She froze where she stood. Had the power just gone out? Or was something else going on?

She held her breath for a few seconds then let it out slowly. Crap! No wonder her co-workers thought she was crazy. Everything seemed like a conspiracy to her. She'd just managed to turn a mere power outage into something much worse in her mind.

She'd heard rumbling off in the distance a few minutes ago. There'd been a thunderstorm threatening all day. Lightning must have struck a pole nearby.

Feeling her way along the counter to her miscellaneous drawer, she opened it and started to feel around for a penlight. She'd use it to help find the bigger battery-operated lantern in the hall closet.

A low, out-of-place creak in the hallway shattered the silence, and Liz stopped digging. Oh God! Someone was in her house.

A scream rose in her throat, until a gust of wind buffeted the side of her house, causing another creak. Liz swallowed hard and cursed herself for her stupidity.

Deep thunder rolled in the distance. The storm was coming fast, and with it stronger wind.

She released a shaky breath. She was alone in the house. Alone and afraid of the dark, apparently. "Get a grip on yourself, Liz," she mumbled, beginning to forage again for the flashlight. Where the heck was it?

Thunder rumbled again. Closer this time. She'd almost convinced herself everything was okay when the hall floorboard creaked again, a sound that rang like a buzzer in her brain.

This time, it definitely hadn't been wind settling the house.

Those particular floorboards creaked only when someone stood in that hallway between the kitchen and the front door. And, she thought she smelled a faint odor of men's cologne.

Just feet away from her.

Her arms iced over, and her throat tightened. She streaked toward the back door off the kitchen.

"Stop, bitch," a deep male voice shouted. Out of the dark, a hand snagged the back of her shirt, then grabbed her hair and yanked her backward.

She screamed. It echoed through the house. But no one else lived here anymore. No one could help. She sobbed. "What do you want?" Her hands went to her hair to try to relieve the yanking pressure on her scalp. "Let me go."

His arms wrapped her in a tight squeeze and he ground himself against her and let out a guttural, disgusting sound.

If this was the person who'd been tormenting her for the last year, his incursions had escalated beyond mere vandalism. She was in deep trouble, and if she wanted to live, she'd better start fighting. Now!

She managed to smash him on the chin with her elbow. He grunted but locked her arms at her sides so she couldn't do it again. It was dark enough that she couldn't see anything but an outline. She wouldn't be able to identify him even if she survived this attack.

His fingers dug into the tender flesh on her arms, and she gritted her teeth against crying out again. No way did she intend to do anything to make this easy for him, but she'd have to be smart. She'd have to find a way to fight him off.

"Been waiting awhile for this," he said in a husky, nearly panting voice that scared her beyond words.

"I've got a present for you, little lady," the voice grated in her ear. He made a lurid, sexual sound, and then laughed. That laugh scared her more than the attack itself.

"Oh God, help me!" she screamed, before his hand clamped over her mouth. Tears sprang to her eyes as her chest exploded into a burning ball of pain from lack of oxygen. He'd started panting in her ear again—and then someone knocked on the front door.

He cursed under his breath and lessened his hold just enough for her to gasp for breath.

Until then, she'd barely registered that someone was insistently knocking on the front door.

"Shut up if you know what's good for you." He dragged her to the far corner of the kitchen.

A key grated in the lock, and the door opened. "Liz, are you in here?"

Only one person had a key to her house. The one person she trusted enough to have a key. Maggie Cranston, her next-door neighbor.

No, Maggie, run! Don't come in here! The unvoiced scream filled her head, but her captor kept his hand so tight over her mouth she felt she wasn't getting enough air.

Maggie advanced slowly, holding a lantern. She must have seen the power go out. Meanwhile, Liz's attacker pulled her farther back into the shadows. "Keep quiet, or you're both in trouble," he whispered.

"I saw the lights go out over here and thought I'd better come over and check on you," Maggie said in a perplexed voice. She paused, then took several steps down the hallway. "Liz? Where are you, dear?" She took a right turn, and the light disappeared into the living room.

With that vile hand clamped over her mouth, Liz couldn't shout, but she did try to struggle. Maggie started into the hallway again.

"Damn it all to hell!" he grated in her ear, then without warning, he shoved her down onto the kitchen floor and dashed out the back door.

Liz hit the floor hard, but managed to break her fall with her hands. Glass cut into her left palm. Her throat felt raw, and she couldn't make a noise.

Maggie had heard the commotion and rushed into the kitchen, bathing Liz in lantern light.

"Help." Liz barely managed to make her voice heard.

"Oh my dear! What happened? Have you broken something?" Maggie's facial features appeared ghoulish in the shadowy glow of her flashlight. Broken glass crunched when she set the flashlight on the floor beside Liz. "You're bleeding. You've cut your hand."

"Call the police," Liz managed to croak out.

"What?" Maggie looked bewildered.

Liz nodded vigorously, clutching her throat. "You just scared off an intruder! He was in my house waiting for me to come home."

"You're kidding." Maggie's chubby hand flew to her mouth. "When your lights went out and no one else's did, I thought you'd blown a breaker. I wasn't sure you knew where the fuse box was, so I came to help."

Liz rubbed her sore throat. What would he have done to her if Maggie hadn't shown up? She shivered at the thought. "Lucky for me you noticed."

Maggie helped her up and onto a kitchen chair. Her motherly fingers smoothed her mussed hair. "Stay right there, Liz, I'm going to call the police."

"Would you lock the back door first?"

"Oh geez!" Maggie ran to the door and pulled it shut and snapped the chain in place.

Not that locked doors had kept out the intruder the first time. How had he gotten into her home?

Maggie kept Liz grounded while they waited for the cops. Somehow it felt like it took forever, but a female officer arrived within twenty minutes and introduced herself as Officer Spencer. "Tell me what happened," she said, holding a pen over her notepad.

Liz quickly gave her a rundown, and afterward her teeth and jaw ached from trying not to panic all over again.

"I see," the tall woman said, looking her over from head to toe. "Did he steal anything?"

"I don't think stealing was on his agenda," Liz said, unable to keep the quiver out of her voice.

"Oh, dear me." Maggie's hand was over her mouth again, and her eyes began watering. She had such a tender heart.

"I know how terrifying it must've been for you to encounter someone in your house, but most likely you interrupted a break-in," the officer said.

"No way in hell," Liz ground out and ran her hands through her tangled hair. "Given all the other things that have happened to me lately, this attack was personal." She couldn't believe the officer had just said that.

"Just take a minute to assess your situation, Ms. Davis," Officer Spencer began in a trained voice. "It's completely normal for a person to assume the worst when they come across an intruder, but sometimes intruders just want to get out of the house when they're caught. Maybe you got in his way? And, there have been a few break-ins in the neighborhood the last few weeks. If this is the same intruder, I don't think you have to worry about him coming back." She held up a hand and waved her pen, still lodged between two fingers. "Not that it's not a scary occurrence, but you need to understand it likely wasn't anything personal."

Liz couldn't believe what she was hearing. "But my brake line was cut last week. Why would a thief do that?"

The officer frowned. "Did you report it?"

Feeling defensive, Liz shot her an angry look. "Of course I did, and I've reported a few other incidents that happened over the last year. Someone is stalking me."

"Just a moment, I'd like to get your records on the brake incident," Officer Spencer said, pulling out her cell phone.

Surely they'd delve deeper into the incidents happening to her this time. Two attempts on her life. Wouldn't that be a little too obvious to ignore?

Officer Spencer stepped into the living room to make her call. She returned a couple of minutes later. "I've checked on the details of the brake incident. Apparently, there was no evidence of tampering." She regarded Liz. "Am I right?"

Liz wanted to scream. She was right! Damn it. She nodded.

"While I realize this incident seems connected to you, there's nothing to indicate it wasn't a random occurrence. As I said, there have been a lot of break-ins in the neighborhood recently. This guy was probably getting ready to rob you when you came in and spoiled his plans."

Liz's arms and legs felt like lead. Her attack hadn't been a foiled robbery, but there was no chance she'd convince the police of that. "So I've been the victim of two random crimes in two weeks? And it's all one big coincidence?"

"I know you want it to be something else, Ms. Davis, but you most likely caught someone attempting to rob you. I suggest you get your locks changed and consider staying with a friend for a while if you don't feel safe."

Easy to tell Officer Spencer had talked to Chief Hanlon. He'd been making her feel like a nut case since day one. Poor little distraught woman who couldn't face up to her parents' death. It wasn't that!

"And if you're wrong?" Something was going on, and no one believed her. Certainly not the police. She had little recourse. It was time she looked after herself.

* * * * *

A week later Liz pulled her car into the driveway after searching for work all morning long and finding nothing. She hadn't slept well last night, and she was exhausted and hungry. At least nothing else had happened since the attack in her kitchen. Maybe it really was over.

She bent over in the foyer and started to remove her shoes but remembered she wanted to check on a tiny robin's nest precariously situated in the ancient oak tree in her backyard. She might have no plans for her life, but she had come up with a solution to save the nest. If it still looked like it might fall, she'd get the ladder out of the garage and take a chance at straightening it. If she wore gloves, maybe the momma bird wouldn't mind.

No time like the present. She slipped her shoe back on. Lunch could wait. She strode through the house and out the back door.

The gnarled oak's leaves at the back of her house rustled in the warm June breeze. The scent of lilacs from her neighbor's yard drifted over the tall hedge between the two houses. Rethinking her choice of shoes, she tiptoed carefully across the yard in her high heels, trying not to sink into the lawn.

Standing directly under the largest branch of the old tree, she noted the shaky little brown nest sitting in the crook of the branch. It hadn't fallen. Yet.

She'd just stretched her arms up to see if she could reach the nest in the lower branch without a ladder when an earsplitting noise exploded behind her, followed immediately by a powerful blast that hit her like a hot-air tsunami and blew her off her feet.

She smelled singed hair and frizzled leaves when she pushed herself out of the hedge near the oak tree. Her hair hung in front of her eyes as she tried to untangle her clothes from the branches of the damaged hedge.

What had just happened?

Ears still ringing, she slowly turned to see. Her home! Her little home, which had held precious memories of her parents, gone. Or, at least not much was left. Jagged bits of the roof jutted toward the sky like desiccated whale bones being lapped by growing heat and fire. The rest of it lay in mangled, burning pieces scattered around the yard. Increasing ugly red and orange flames roared and the fire grew in intensity.

Stunned and unable to comprehend totally what had just happened, she stared at the horror in front of her until she heard shouting from her neighbors over the din of her house being roasted. She instantly hunkered down, and reality sank in.

Someone had very nearly killed her this time. Would the police believe it was another accident? Would she have a chance to convince them before whoever did this got to her?

She had to run. To get away and figure this out.

It took that long to make her decision. If she disappeared, maybe everyone would think she died in that explosion.

Someone had deliberately blown up her house.
There was no doubt now.
Someone wanted her dead.

Chapter Two

Jake Johnston smelled the aroma of bacon before he even got close to the kitchen. Hiring a housekeeper five years ago had been the best thing he ever did. At the time, Ada Dawson had needed the money during her husband's illness. Her husband had gotten better, and Ada had continued to work for him. He tugged at the waist of his jeans. Good thing he worked out, otherwise he'd be putting weight on.

"Morning, Ada."

She turned and smiled at him. "Coffee, dear?"

"Please." He sat at the table and snapped open his paper. "Your coffee's the best in the city."

"Considering that you practically live on the stuff, that's quite a compliment."

He took a tentative drink of the hot brew and sighed.

"Eggs today, sweetie?"

"No, thanks. Just toast, please."

"French toast?" She always tried to get eggs into him for breakfast. She obviously wasn't worried about his cholesterol.

"Sure, French toast'll be fine."

Ada hummed as she whisked three eggs and milk in a bowl while Jake read his paper.

"Have I told you about Liz, the neighbor next door?" Ada began while she put the egg-covered bread into the hot frying pan then dished up the sizzling bacon from the other pan.

Ack! Jake feigned deafness. He'd seen the woman who had moved in next door. She was very pretty, and Ada constantly played matchmaker.

"She just moved in last week. Surely you've seen her?" Ada wiped her hands on her apron and peered at him over her burgundy-rimmed eyeglasses, a tactic she used whenever she wanted to be sure she had his full attention.

"No, I haven't seen her." Why'd he say that? His shoulders shrugged around his ears. Why even try to avoid the inevitable? He sighed and took another long drink of his dark brew.

"She's single, you know." Ada waited for a response, and from his peripheral vision he could see her hands on her hips. He bit back a grin.

He should be used to her matchmaking by now. "Yeah?" He focused on his paper and didn't look up.

"She asked me yesterday if I knew of anyone who could help fix her inside garage door. You know which one I mean, between the garage and the house." She set four thick slices of golden French toast between him and his paper. "She's a little nervous that she can't lock her door at night. I told her about the break-ins up the street last year."

He cringed inwardly.

"She asked the landlord to fix her door, but he's out of town. Can't blame her for being nervous. A girl can't be too careful."

Hell. The poor woman had probably been scared out of her wits by Ada's well-meaning help. He'd have to make a point of securing the door for her today, before Ada unwittingly scared her any further. "I'll go see her after work, Ada," he said in an off-the-cuff voice, hoping she wouldn't gather any meaning from it.

Ada grinned from ear to ear and kissed him on the forehead. He grumbled and ruffled his paper, but they both knew he liked the attention as much as she liked to give it. He'd been adopted as the son she'd never had.

* * * * *

At work that day, Jake kept a close eye on the time. He packed up at four o'clock. Usually he worked later, but he had most of his paperwork done and he felt an obligation to help his next-door neighbor. Especially since Ada had been filling her in on the community's safety issues.

Ada's mouth hung open in fake shock when he entered the kitchen. She held up her wrist and glanced at her aged gold watch. "You're early."

"Surprised?"

"You never come home early."

"Thought I'd fix the neighbor's door," he said.

"Why don't I come over and introduce you two?" she said, sliding off her apron and heading toward the back door.

"No, that's not necessary. Why don't you go home and have a nice weekend with John? I imagine he'd appreciate a early hot dinner tonight, too."

John was her soft spot. She adored her husband, and he'd be the only thing that would break her attention from trying to set Jake up with the unwitting woman next door.

"Good idea." She paused. "You sure I shouldn't come with you to introduce you first?" He nodded vigorously. "No, no. I'll be fine. You get a jumpstart on your weekend."

"Okay. Your dinner is ready in the oven, dear."

"What did you say her name is again?"

"Liz Davidson. She's young and single. A real looker, too."

He grinned at Ada and shook his head when she winked at him. "I'm not in the market, Ada."

She pulled a face at him and reached for her lightweight coat. "All right. See you in the morning."

He waited until her car drove off before he went anywhere near the neighbor's place. No sense tempting matchmaker fate. Since it was a warm day, he'd changed into a pair of shorts and a T-shirt. With toolbox in hand, he crossed their side-by-side driveways and rapped a few times on the front door.

"Who is it?" he heard from inside. Yep, he was right. Ada had scared her.

"Name's Jake. We haven't met yet," he said. Could she hear him? He spoke louder. "I'm Jake Johnston, your next-door neighbor. Ada said you could use my help." He heard scraping and something heavy being moved.

A draught of cool air hit him as she opened the door. The interior of the house was so dark behind her that for a moment all he could see was her silhouette. The odor of something freshly baked greeted his nostrils. It smelled great.

As his vision adjusted, he clearly saw Liz Davidson. She indeed fit the "looker" moniker Ada had given her. She was even prettier close up. Long thick blond hair framed her face. Wide dark brown eyes stared back at him. She wore shorts and a tank top, fluffy pink pigs on her feet. He grinned. He liked the pigs.

"I'm Li...uh, Liz Davidson." She held out her hand.

He took her hand then let it go quickly. "Just call me Jake. I should get right to work fixing your garage door while it's still light outside." She seemed scared, all right. Because of Ada? He sure as hell hoped not.

"Thank you so much. I've been a little nervous."

"Yes, well, about that," he began, "I don't think you should let Ada worry you. We live in a great neighborhood."

Liz smiled weakly. "It's nice of you to offer your expertise."

He adjusted the toolbox in his left hand and followed her down the hall past the living room and through the kitchen. Expert he wasn't. He just hoped he didn't make a fool of himself in the repairman department.

On his way through he noticed thick living room drapes were tightly drawn, letting very little light through at the back of the house. The kitchen felt brighter with sheer curtains and a nice breeze billowing into the room through the screened window. A coconut cream pie sat on the counter, and coffee brewed in the pot.

It took only a second to see that the doorknob had simply worked its way loose and two screws had gone missing. He found the right-sized screws in his toolbox and started repairing the lock. He'd nearly finished when a soft, flowery scent let him know she was nearby. He inhaled and turned to find her leaning over him. She had the cutest freckles. For one insane moment, he wondered just how far below the neckline of her tank top her freckles went. He straightened and took a deep breath. Get a grip, man.

"Is it bad?" she asked.

"No, not at all. I've readjusted the lock housing and replaced the screws. You can lock it now." He replaced his tools and stood to leave.

* * * * *

Being unable to lock her door at night felt like an invitation to her worst nightmare, and since her landlord had gone away for a few days, she'd had no choice but to accept help from her handsome next-door neighbor. Not something she wanted to have to contend with. She needed to remain anonymous. The more people who met her, the bigger the risk that they'd figure out who she was if they saw her face in the news.

She'd tried to avoid Ada in the beginning. But the woman was persistent, and truth be told, Liz hadn't been fast enough. Plus, she hadn't wanted to make the older woman suspicious.

Looking at Jake, Liz thought about the way Ada had described him. She'd actually expected some sort of slim workaholic loner, not the muscled, good-looking guy standing in front of her.

Besides, she should be safe here in New Brunswick. The Canadian province bordering Maine had been the closest and quickest escape. Would anyone suspect she'd left the country? She'd hidden her tracks well enough not to be found; at least, she hoped she had. She sighed inwardly. As long as her two neighbors didn't identify her from news reports, and she didn't think they got all that much news from Maine here in Fredericton. She'd spent a couple of summers here as a kid, so she wasn't totally unfamiliar with the area.

"Can I offer you a coffee?" she asked, shuffling her slippered feet. The sooner she got him out of here, the better, but first she had to pretend to be gracious. "A glass of iced tea?"

"No, thanks."

She'd been on the run for a week. Within minutes of her house blowing up, she'd withdrawn as much money as she could from the bank machine around the corner from her house and had taken the first bus out of town. She'd always kept extra money in her wallet along with her passport, both of which she'd had with her in her backpack purse when she walked out into the backyard. Lucky.

Now here she stood, staring at a neighbor who looked like he wanted to get away from her as fast as possible, and that made her feel better about him. If he'd shown too much interest, she'd have been suspicious of him, too.

"Ada tells me that you work for the city," she said, trying to make an effort at being friendly when she really wanted him to leave.

"Yeah, I'm a meteorologist," he said. "Because of that I work odd hours, depending on what's happening in the skies."

"Really," she said, trying to sound more interested than she felt. Normally, she'd ask questions, but she had other things on her mind.

She frowned. An uneasy feeling crept through her. "I wouldn't have bothered you but I just don't like sleeping in a house with unlocked doors. I come from a neighborhood where it's not wise to do that." She cringed at her stupid comment, giving him an opening to ask where she'd come from.

"What neighborhood is that?" he asked.

Now what to do? He most likely wouldn't connect her to the splashy news story in all the Maine papers about the explosion. But she decided to avoid any discussion of Maine, just in case. Mercifully none of her neighbors had been injured. "Toronto."

"I see what you mean. Toronto is a place to lock your doors."

She sighed. Thankfully he didn't ask her where in Toronto, because she'd never been there in her life, but she'd heard her uncle talk about it. Lucky for her, she didn't have a strong Maine accent. She'd been living in Europe before her father had retired to Maine, so she hadn't developed their lovely down-east manner of speaking.

He leaned one arm against the counter top. You don't have to worry about this neighborhood. Nothing ever happens here."

"I'm glad to hear that," she said.

"You've got a good computer there," he said. Being new, the computer still had the plastic sticker on the front, listing its software and hardware information.

She hesitated awkwardly. "Thanks."

"Is this why you're often up late? Do you work at home?"

She frowned at him. She couldn't blame him for being curious. After all, at her age, most women had to work to support themselves. He must be wondering about that. Still, she didn't like the fact that he'd been watching her that closely.

"Oh no! It's not what you think. When I have to work the late shift and get home in the wee hours…" A muscle worked in his jaw. "Yours is the only other house with lights still on."

The silence between them grew deafening before she finally said, "I really must thank you for your help. It'll be good to know my door is safely locked at night." She moved out of the kitchen toward the front door. Fortunately, he followed. She'd exhausted her ability to lie for another second—he had to go.

He rubbed the back of his neck and switched the heavy toolbox from one hand to the other, but lingered inside her front door.

"Seriously, call if you need anything. I'm more than happy to help out," he said and handed her a card with his phone number on it.

Even though she thanked him, she made sure her tone said, Thanks, but no, thanks. "I'm fine here," she lied. She opened the door wide enough for him to leave.

His forehead furrowed, but he took the hint. "Anyway, welcome to the neighborhood." He smiled and extended his hand to her.

She gave his hand a weak shake then hustled him onto the doorstep.

The minute he left, Liz locked the door and strode back to the kitchen and let out a long, shaky breath. Maybe she should have been nicer. And she probably had made him even more curious by acting the way she had.

And she'd almost blurted her real name out when they first met. Not that there was much difference between Davis and Davidson, but she figured she'd be able to cover up her error if she said the wrong name. She'd have to be on her guard around people. Anyway, she wouldn't have to worry about him coming around again after the way she'd just treated him. Hopefully, he'd go out of his way to avoid her from now on.

She plunked onto her computer chair and keyed in her password. Her screen illuminated, and she began scanning the news. Police in Bangor still thought she'd died in the explosion but were actively searching the burned ashes of the house for her remains. More than likely, the fact that there was no body in the house would come out any day now and her picture would be flashed all over the local media.

She probably didn't have much time left to try to figure out who wanted her dead.

She sighed and closed her eyes against the pictures of the remains of her home. When she'd read that the police and fire chief thought that the explosion might have been an accident, she wanted to scream. She'd heard two separate blasts that day. The newspapers had indicated that she kept old paint and oily rags in the basement. Hah! What a lie! And they indicated she had a gas heater in her spare room. Never. Ever.

It seemed that whoever blew up her house had known what they were doing. They'd made it look completely accidental. She shivered as the fear of being stalked by an unknown assailant gripped her once again. She mustn't let her guard down, even though she'd moved hundreds of miles away and he most likely wouldn't find her.

By the time Liz crawled into bed that night, she was dead tired but feeling a little better. With the garage door safely dead-bolted, she might even sleep. She'd written Jake's phone number on a pad of paper and put it beside the phone next to her bed before tucking his card into her purse. Just in case.

Chapter Three

After her first good night's sleep in ages, Liz twisted her hair into a bun and pulled a ball cap on to cover it. Before she could chicken out, she started the late-model car she'd bought for cash the day before and backed out of the driveway without any idea where she planned to go. She ended up downtown and parked near the museum, then wandered the hiking trail for a while before choosing a park bench off the main trail overlooking the ever-changing views of the river. Rowing teams and the occasional sailboat slid by on the calm water. Changing currents and wind created patterns on the water that mesmerized her long enough to almost forget.

Reluctantly, she returned home after stopping for groceries. She'd grabbed two grocery bags from the back seat of the old car and shut the door with her hip. She'd have to mete out her grocery funds. She had enough money to last her for a while, but it wouldn't hold out forever. That meant that sooner or later she'd have to get a job, and to do that she'd have to go back to the US, maybe to another state to find work.

Her neighbor pulled into his driveway and hopped out of his Jeep and waved. "Hey there. Out shopping, I see."

She looked down at her plastic bags then yanked off her oversize sunglasses and baseball cap and shoved them in her pocket. She nodded.

"Wow, you must really like shopping, because, lady, you look just about like you're on cloud nine." He crossed to her yard with one finger hooked onto his belt.

She frowned.

"Nice to see color in your cheeks."

She stiffened. She definitely needed to avoid him.

"Yes, well, I'd better get these things inside," she said, edging away. And she needed to ignore his spicy aftershave, his white dress shirt with rolled-up sleeves that accentuated his tanned good looks and those blue jeans riding low on his trim hips.

"Right," he said, but a crease formed between his eyebrows. "I have some yard work to do, anyway. See you later."

She stepped inside and shut out her neighbor who, to her dismay, still watched her from near the back bumper of her old car.

She leaned against the front door and closed her eyes. His scent lingered in her memory, and against her will, her heart registered those gorgeous blue eyes that had watched her with concern. She had to ignore the urge to get to know him better. She couldn't afford to trust anyone until she found out what the hell was going on.

Heat built into the night. An early summer storm loomed, and she tossed and turned all night long. Images of her house exploding and heat from the burning flames haunted her dreams. She woke in a sweat. There was no air conditioning or fans in the house, and being too afraid to open her bedroom window to let the cool night air in didn't help.

Now in the solitude of this rented place, she suddenly feared her attacker might have the resources to find her, to learn that she'd used her passport to exit the country.

And, any day now, the arson inspectors would be advising the police that there were no human remains in the burned embers of her house. She had little time, and so far she hadn't been able to find out a single thing on the computer about why the house had exploded. Her father had retired from the military. Maybe it was connected to his job? Did someone have a grudge against him? There was no doubt in her mind that her parents had been murdered even though their accident couldn't be explained by the police. Finally, the investigators had suggested her father had fallen asleep at the wheel at three in the afternoon! Not damned likely. But why target them? Why her?

The kitchen felt almost cool this morning, quite a switch from the excessive heat last night. Rain pounded on the roof and showered the windows in steady gusts.

Yesterday had been a perfect day, but today the continual drizzle dampened her already dark mood. Heaving a sigh, she glanced through the bay windows in the kitchen alcove.

Unexpectedly, a shadowy figure ran past her window and made for the back yard. Her muscles tightened, and she bit back a scream. Had she really seen someone out there? She went to the living room and stared through the windowpanes, hoping to prove herself wrong. At first, everything looked normal. Until a figure darted from the hedge to the willow tree and disappeared at the back of the lot.

Oh my God! She started to shake. Instantly, she grabbed the phone and dialed Jake's number. His phone rang and rang. Of course, he was probably still in bed. It was only five thirty.

"Hello?" He sounded half-asleep.

"Jake, it's Liz, next door. Can you come right over?" Her voice hitched when she tried to hold back the emotion clawing at her throat.

"What? Who?" He wasn't awake yet.

"Liz . Your next-door neighbor. I just saw someone slinking around in my backyard. I'm really scared."

He inhaled sharply. "Be right there. Don't worry."

She pressed one shaking hand over her mouth. Get hold of yourself, Liz. How are you ever going to keep yourself alive if you fall apart every time something happens? Besides, she'd called the cavalry, and he'd be at her door any second.

Wait! Should she get out of the house? Could there be a bomb outside the window? Oh God! That creaking hallway floorboard sprang to mind. If that happened now, she'd scream bloody murder and run out the door onto the front lawn…if she made it that far. Heat swept over her, followed by an icy chill.

Sudden pounding on the front door made her nearly exit her skin.

"Liz. Let me in!" Jake hollered and pounded again. "Are you okay in there?"

It took forever to unlatch the bolts and chains to let him inside.

He grabbed her shoulders and squeezed gently. "There's no need to worry. I'll check it out," he said in a calming voice. She'd sounded pretty panicked on the phone.

He had obviously thrown on his jeans since they weren't completely buttoned. His hair hadn't been combed, but it still looked good. His expression proved he'd taken her call very seriously. "What happened?"

"There's someone in the backyard. I think he was just looking in…in my kitchen window." She clasped her hands together to quell the trembling.

He reached out and squeezed her shoulder. "I'll check it out. I won't be long. You stay here. Lock your door."

"No! Don't leave me." She squeezed her eyes shut. She was doomed. This kind of fear would definitely get her killed.

He gave her shoulder another light squeeze and waited for her to open her eyes.

"Not to worry. I'll check the back yard to see if anyone's still there."

She nodded. "Be careful."

She watched him through the windows on the first floor. The rain had lessened to a drizzle but she still felt terrible about making him wander around out there barefoot through the wet grass and rain.

He couldn't have been more thorough. He covered every inch of her yard.

At the back of the lot he climbed through the bushes and disappeared behind the willow tree in the same direction as the stranger who'd been in her yard. She waited for what seemed like an eternity until he reappeared.

When he returned he was drenched. "Did you see anything?" she asked, handing him a towel.

He wiped his face and hair. "I found the culprit."

"You did?" She swallowed hard. "Who…who is it?"

"Mr. Armadale next door was in the bushes with his little dog Suzette. Apparently, he sneaks out early in the morning because the dear little poodle likes to do her business only in your backyard." He sounded irritated. "I told him that he'd given you quite a fright, and he's feeling rather badly right now."

She let out a shaky breath and leaned against the wall next to the door. "Oh."

"I can understand why that would scare you, Liz," he began. "But I'm not sure why it terrified you."

"I…I don't know. It just startled me, that's all," she mumbled and looked away, unable to meet his gaze in case he figured her out.

"You're sure? There's nothing more? I mean, when I got here a few minutes ago, you were terrified, Liz. I saw the look on your face!"

She didn't need to make him even more curious about her, but she'd asked him for help and now she'd have to do damage control. "Don't be silly. This is a new neighborhood for me, and besides, I'm not used to having people lurking about in my backyard at ungodly hours of the morning."

His arm brushed hers, and goose bumps broke out instantly. "Jake, you're freezing! I'll make you a cup of coffee. Breakfast, if you like."

"Coffee sounds good, but no breakfast, thanks." His wet feet squeaked on the hardwood floor as he padded down the hall behind her.

He sat at the table while she got two mugs out of the cupboard. "What about you?" he asked. "You okay now?"

She stiffened for a second but forced herself to relax. She spun around with a cup in each hand and laughed lightly. "Really, I feel so stupid now that I know that old man and his poodle were my culprits." She filled the cups and put his in front of him. "I'm so sorry I woke you up for such a foolish thing."

"It wasn't foolish. Mr. Armadale should have known better. You probably could report him if you want to. It's illegal to let an animal do their business in a neighbor's yard. He could be fined by the city."

"Oh gosh, no!" Damn, she'd overdone the reaction again. She knew it the instant his expression grew more serious. He didn't say anything, and she had a feeling that was worse than his curiosity.

* * * * *

On the way home in his bare feet twenty minutes later, Jake stepped on a sharp stone. He hopped around and uttered a few choice words under his breath. What the hell was he doing? When he'd arrived this morning and saw the state Liz was in, his gut sense had told him she was in trouble. The thought abused wife on the run had surfaced, but then that hadn't felt right. Normally, he could figure people out, but this one was a mystery.

At the sight of Ada's car in his driveway, he checked his watch. "Shoot." He'd wanted to get home before she arrived and found out he'd been at Liz's place. No matter what he told Ada about why he'd gone to help Liz, Ada would come to the wrong conclusion. She'd go into full-on cupid mode.

He couldn't tell her that Liz had been terrified and shaking like a leaf when he got there. Ada would have been over there trying to shake the poor girl down for information and then expect him to do whatever it took to help defray the damage she'd done. He had the feeling helping his neighbor wouldn't be easy.

The screen door creaked as he opened it, and Ada's expression said it all when he stepped into the kitchen wearing nothing but his jeans and thin T-shirt. In fact, she was speechless for about two seconds.

"Where have you been, dressed like that?" Her eyes flicked knowingly toward Liz's house. He sighed.

"Just went to check on something for our neighbor." He didn't meet his caring housekeeper's gaze as he wiped his wet feet on the floor mat.

"Needed a cup of sugar?" she asked suggestively, looking at his empty hands. "Never mind, you don't have to tell me a thing. After all, I'm only your housekeeper. It's none of my business."

She was a helluva lot more than that to him, and she knew it. She didn't often use guilt to get information out of him, though. He bit back a smile.

"Let me just say this, Ada. It's not what you're obviously thinking." He trudged across the kitchen. He stopped and kissed her cheek. "I'm going for a shower."

He heard Ada talking to herself as he mounted the stairs.

The steaming hot water felt extra good this morning. It had been pretty cold when he was out stalking the neighbor and his poodle. The thought of the man sneaking into Liz's yard to let his poodle do his business was pretty disgusting. He rubbed shampoo into his hair. That still didn't explain the fear that Liz had obviously experienced. He'd swear she'd been terrified.

Twenty minutes later, dressed and ready for work, he met Ada in the kitchen. She poured coffee into his cup and handed it to him. Before she could start subtly quizzing him, he took her by surprise by saying, "Eggs, please. Over easy. No, make that two eggs and sausage and toast. Oh yeah, throw in some of your strawberry freezer jam, too, please." He figured telling her he wanted eggs would not only please her but keep her occupied. She'd have less time to grill him. He opened the paper and held it up.

Somehow, he'd managed to get away without telling Ada anything.

By four o'clock he could barely sit still. He'd never experienced a workday that took so long to pass. The reason for his distraction worried him even more. No way should he be thinking about his lovely next-door neighbor and the way her silky blond hair framed her huge, terrified brown eyes.

Or maybe he was interested in her for the wrong reasons? A woman in freaking jeopardy seemed to ring all of his come-to-the-rescue bells, whether he liked it or not. Dating women with issues hadn't worked out so well for him in the past.

When his shift ended, he headed home. As he tried to persuade himself to forget his neighbor, it exasperated him that her image kept popping into his mind.

It had been a weird day from the moment he got the phone call and ran next door in nothing but a pair of jeans and T-shirt.

He stepped into his house expecting Ada to be fully armed with questions he'd escaped earlier.

"Hi, Jake! Have a good day?" Ada smiled at him then wiped off the kitchen counter.

"Great thanks." He waited a minute. Not a single question ensued. She rarely missed a chance to be cupid. He was still wondrous when she got ready and left.

After dinner, he took his coffee outside and sat on a bright red Adirondack chair on his back deck. The way he instantly glanced across the small white picket fence to her yard irked him to no end.

Of course, she wasn't there. Her car hadn't even been in her driveway when he got home. As if on cue, he heard its rattling engine drawing closer.

He shouldn't do it, but he did. He got up and made for the front of the house.

She wore that silly baseball cap that hid her beautiful hair and those gawd-awful sunglasses that she wore whenever she drove the old rattletrap. Like last time, she took off the cap and glasses and stuffed them into her pocket the minute she saw him. Warning bells that had been tinkling in his brain were getting louder, but he shoved his fears to the background.

Hiding his building apprehension, he held up a hand and waved. She didn't look pleased to see him, but she still stopped and waited for him.

"Evening. Did our wayward neighbor apologize?" Jake tipped his head toward Mr. Armadale's house.

"He did," she said.

There was no sign of the fear in her eyes this morning. Had he imagined it before?

"In fact, I'm feeling rather stupid for waking you up this morning," she said.

"No need. It isn't exactly normal for your next-door neighbor to sneak around in your yard with his dog at that hour of the morning. I have the feeling he won't be doing it again, though."

He noticed a plastic bag jammed with newspapers on the passenger seat of her car. How much news did one person need? "Can I help carry anything in?"

She instantly dove for the car door and grabbed the bag before he could make a move. Okay, she wanted to be left alone. She tucked the plastic bag with the newspapers under her arm while he followed her into the kitchen. Her actions wouldn't have meant much if she hadn't tried so hard to keep those papers from him. She crossed to the computer and slipped the papers into the desk drawer. Why would she be so secretive about buying newspapers?

"How was your day today?" she asked.

"Pretty standard." The way she looked at him, so innocent and big-eyed, brought his curiosity to a halt and started his brain overheating. He needed to go home. Now!

She smiled at him, and his heart rate picked up a notch.

She obviously didn't realize the effect she had on him, standing there with her soft-green shorts and skimpy T-shirt molded to her luscious body. He needed the sanctity of his bachelor pad and quick.

That way he'd keep his nose out of her troubles.

* * * * *

After her experiences in Bangor, she'd had it up to her eyeballs with people who wouldn't believe her. In fact, she'd be dead right now if she hadn't gone outside to check on that bird's nest, and the cops were probably still calling it an accident. Bile rose in her throat. The irony of it was the bird's nest hadn't budged during the explosion. It had been secure all along.

She didn't want Jake to get curious about her, though. She'd have to play it cooler than she had so far. She swallowed hard. Was it a crime to pretend to be dead? Probably.

If only she knew how to contact Uncle Brody. He was on an oil rig somewhere in the Persian Gulf, and she had no idea which company he worked for or how to contact him. As some sort of important petroleum consultant, he moved around often.

Normally, he visited at least once a year. As far as she knew, Uncle Brody didn't even know about her parents' deaths yet. She had tried to find a phone number, anything that would lead her to Brody. She'd thought it odd that her mother hadn't had his phone number written in her address book. If the number had been somewhere in the house, it was lost forever now, along with every picture and keepsake that would have helped to keep her parents alive in her memory.

She wondered how many oil companies existed in the Persian Gulf. She could have started writing letters to every company over there, but that would take forever.

Brody had always been a devoted uncle. She adored him and missed him immensely. She needed him even more now that she was all alone. But she was in hiding, and if he were to look for her, he wouldn't find her.

Feeling frustrated and lonely, she decided to do some laundry to stop her overworked mind from completely losing it.

She opened the basement door, flipped on the light and started downstairs. On the third step, she'd barely placed her foot down when it slipped out from under her. She tumbled the rest of the way down the stairs, slamming her shin into the wooden handrail post before hitting the concrete floor at the bottom.

Pain seared her flesh, and she didn't move at first. She stayed there on the cold, hard concrete, too afraid to move until every pain and bump announced itself.

Finally, with slow, careful movements, she tested her limbs before she attempted to push herself up.

Ouch, her chest burned. It hurt to breathe. She must have pulled a muscle or cracked a rib. She saw a bluish lump rising on her right shin. That hurt like the dickens.

Why had she slipped? She glanced back up the wooden steps and bit her lip against the pain. She was lucky not to have broken her neck.

With effort, she climbed back up the steps. Just before reaching the spot where she'd slipped, she eyed a little puddle of wet-looking black fluid reflecting the overhead light.

She squinted at the ceiling above it. An oil pipe crossed the ceiling above the step. The pipe had a fresh, tiny globule of oil about to drip from it. Funny, she hadn't noticed that before. The oil company must have filled the tank while she was out. There must be a hole in the pipe.

She'd make sure to mention that to the landlord. And, really, you'd think he would have told her he was having the tank filled.

When she made it to the kitchen, she got out a small plastic bottle of acetaminophen from the cupboard, threw a couple of caplets into her mouth at the same time and swallowed them down with water.

The living room sofa appeared extremely far away as she hobbled toward it. She settled herself back and rested her head against the padded arm. Throbbing nerve endings made it hard to think straight. She closed her eyes and tried to tamp down the pain.

At some point she'd fallen asleep, because when she awoke it was dark.

She moved, and pain shrieked through her. Her leg hurt the worst. She pushed herself into a sitting position. Her stomach rumbled in hunger.

She moved her leg and gasped out loud. Knives of agony shot through her shin. She didn't even want to try to put any weight on it, but she knew she had to get up, at least to get some ice for it. An ugly lump had risen dramatically and had already turned purple. With each step, knives of pain assaulted her leg. In the kitchen, she shoved ice cubes into a bag and made her way back to the couch. By the time she sat down, she was completely exhausted.

The ice felt good on her shin. She took turns laying the cold compress on one sore spot, then another.

What a wretched time for her to have a stupid accident. While trying to protect herself from being hurt, she'd very nearly done herself in. She moaned in self-disgust. Whoever wanted her dead, would probably love it if she finished herself off without any outside help.

The ice melted quickly, and before long, she set the sealed plastic bag of ice water onto the floor beside the couch and closed her heavy eyelids again.

Hours later the pain of her injuries burgeoned to life and woke her. She'd made it through the night at least.

Her shin wasn't quite as swollen as it had been. One good thing.

It still hurt to inhale, and she had a couple of dandy-looking bruises on her arms, and her tailbone hurt, but as she stood and tried to put weight on her shin, she heaved a sigh of relief. Yes, it still hurt, but it was feeling much better today.

She hobbled to the bathroom and washed up then got herself some toast and more painkillers for breakfast.

Now that she was up and quasi-mobile again, she retrieved the newspapers she'd bought and laid them out on the kitchen table to scan them for any information that might help, especially any news about her house in Bangor and the inspector's findings.

How strange to dread the thought of people discovering she was still alive. Then she thought of poor Maggie, her former next-door neighbor. She'd be distraught. If only she could tell Maggie she'd survived.

Liz cringed. Maggie might hear the news soon enough. When they learned her body wasn't in the ashes, what then? A chill went up her spine.

What then?

Chapter Four

Jake hadn't seen Liz for a few days. There'd been almost no sign of life at her house, except for her lights going on after dark. He frowned. Should he go check on her? Or was this a message that she wanted to be left alone?

No matter what he really wanted to do, the truth was she'd been so damned scared the other morning that he felt he had no choice but to check on her.

He rang her doorbell and waited patiently. He heard movement inside, but she didn't come to the door.

Again, he pushed on the doorbell, leaning on it longer this time. He saw the side panel curtains move slightly. Then latches began to slowly unclick, one after another. Three locks in total.

The door opened and she peered at him through the small crack in the door.

"I haven't seen you for a couple of days," he began. "Just thought I'd check and make sure everything's okay."

"I'm fine," she said.

Her monotone voice made it difficult for him to read her emotions. "Would you be interested in coming over to my place for a cup of coffee?" Did he see her eyes brighten?

"No, I...I can't. I'm rather busy at the moment."

"Liz , why not take a bit of time off work? I rented a movie," he coaxed, wondering what her job could be. She rarely left the house.

"No, thank you," she said, still peering through the crack of the door at him.

"Well, then, why not invite me in?" Something about this felt off. And he was damned sure he was going to find out what it was before he left. "Open the door, Liz. I want to know what's wrong."

Her eyes closed. Then he noticed her white-knuckled grip on the door.

She sighed and opened the door fully before she turned away and limped down the hall into the living room. "Come in."

He followed. "Are you limping? What happened?" She turned, and he gasped at her black and blue arms and legs. She had a nasty-looking bump on her shin, too.

His first reaction was anger. "Who did this to you?"

She snorted. "You won't believe it, but I did this to myself. Well, the house helped."

"What?" He kept looking at her bruises, not sure if he believed her story.

"I fell down the stairs. The oil pipe, strangely enough, runs over the basement stairs. It sprung a leak. I slipped on a patch of oil."

"What did the doctor say? Do you have any broken bones?" It was obviously painful for her to sit down.

* * * * *

She finally got herself settled on the couch. "I don't need to see a doctor." That would be all she'd need! Thankfully, she was fairly certain she hadn't broken any bones.

"You didn't see a doctor?" He sounded amazed. "Why in God's name didn't you at least call me?"

"There was no need to call you. Besides, it happened two days ago. I'm fine."

"You did this to yourself two days ago?"

"Yeah. I'm a bit of a klutz lately."

He looked nice tonight, dressed in a T-shirt that showed off his trim but taut frame and lightweight shorts that accented his other nice features. He smelled good, too. Darn it, she needed to get her mind back to protecting herself.

"Why didn't you call someone to come and help you? A relative or a friend?"

She looked down at her bare toes and pondered that question. She didn't trust anyone at this point, and her parents and Uncle Brody were the only close relatives she had. All she had left was Uncle Brody, and she didn't have a clue how to find him. "I'm not a child, Jake. I can look after myself."

"I'm beginning to wonder about that. Look at you. You look like you've been in a car accident." He sat beside her on the couch and took her hand in his large warm one and said, "Let me put it this way: You should have called someone to stay with you. What if you'd needed to go to the hospital and couldn't make it to the phone? Considering the extent of your injuries, I imagine you were in a lot of pain, and it couldn't have been easy to get around and to feed yourself."

She raised her eyebrows. "I appreciate your concern, but I'm quite capable of looking after myself."

He shook his head and sighed. "Everybody needs help once in a while."

"Okay, I give. Next time I fall down the stairs, I swear I'll give you a call." She sounded snippy. If he kept being so considerate, she might have to burst into tears, and she didn't want that to happen.

"Get up. Put your shoes on," he said in a soft enough voice, but she could tell he was very serious. "I've got a movie and some popcorn next door and..." He frowned at her bruises. "Some aspirin, if you need it."

"No, but thanks." Truth be known, she was tired. She hadn't slept well at all since her fall down the basement stairs. Her aches and pains had kept her awake, but more than that, being incapacitated scared her even more. After all, how could she fend off an attacker if she could barely hobble around the house?

"Leg too sore to walk that far?"

"Something like that."

He stood then picked her up off the couch as if she were a child.

"What are you doing?" She grabbed on to his shoulders.

He smiled down at her. His blue eyes were intense and laced with gold flecks she hadn't noticed before.

"We're going to my place." He hesitated. "That is, unless you insist on staying here all alone with no one to talk to."

Maybe it was the physical contact she couldn't turn down. She'd been so alone. Maybe he was helping her only because she seemed so needy? Understatement of the year. She did need someone to talk to about nothing in particular. Another living person. "Am I too heavy?"

"Light as a feather. We're going then?"

"Okay. But I can walk."

"Good one, Liz! I see you have a sense of humor."

As he opened the door, she dug her fingers into his shoulders unwittingly. "Wait! I need my purse and house key." She hoped her voice didn't sound as shrill to him as it did to her.

"No problem." He turned and lowered her enough so that she could reach out and pick up her purse from the hall table. They exited her place, and she hoped he couldn't feel her trembling.

"Lock the door, please."

He flicked the lock on the doorknob, pulled the door shut with the hand under her bottom, and tried the knob again. "All secure. Ready to go?"

She nodded.

As they entered Jake's house, Liz felt herself relaxing involuntarily. It really felt good to be in different surroundings. He set her on her feet in front of the couch. She sat.

"I'm impressed you're not even out of breath," she said flippantly.

He lowered down onto a chair and scanned her bruises in the brighter illumination of his place. His worried expression made a lump rise in her throat. She hated sympathy because it made her feel sorry for herself. She didn't need that, and it would be a dangerous emotion right now. She had to stay tough, alert and able to look after herself. She swallowed hard.

"What did you have for supper tonight?" he asked. He kept his expression aloof, but there was a twinkle of kindness in his eyes. He probably didn't think she'd noticed.

"Don't worry about me. I had supper."

"What did you have, pray tell?"

She grimaced. "You know. The usual supper stuff."

"Which would be?" He tipped his head as though making sure he could hear her.

"Instant Breakfast." There, she said it. It was no big deal.

"I knew it! Okay, I'm ordering pizza. What toppings do you like?"

"Really, it's not necessary..."

"Maybe not necessary, but humor me, okay?" He knelt on the floor in front of her, his hand resting on her knee. Although he seemed unaware of his hand on her, she felt as if it were burning a brand into her leg. Heat rose in her face.

"Anything," was her answer. But she wasn't positive that her answer had a single thing to do with pizza toppings.

Twenty minutes later, they tucked in, and the pizza tasted delicious. She ate two slices. When they were done, Jake sat on the couch beside her. Instead of watching a movie, he put on some classical music and talked about mundane things, nothing personal. Before she knew it, she was so relaxed her eyelids began to droop.

When she awoke, she found herself stretched out on his sofa with a throw on top of her. He sat in a chair in the corner, reading a book. He lifted his gaze when she moved. "Did you sleep well?

"Sorry. After you stuffed me with pizza, I guess I couldn't stay awake."

"I thought you looked exhausted. I had the feeling you might be having trouble sleeping, so I just let you nod off."

"Very intuitive of you." She pushed herself up and gingerly put weight on her sore leg.

He jumped up and had her in his arms in a flash. "Where do you want to go? Bathroom?"

She grinned at him. "How about you take me home?"

"Oh. Okay." Did she detect regret in his voice?

As they crossed from his yard to hers, she said, "I can just imagine what the neighbors must be saying about us. They'll be having a field day. First, you're seen coming out of my place at an ungodly hour in the morning in nothing but jeans and a T-shirt. And now you're carrying me home in the middle of the night. Sorry to put you in a position like this, Jake."

Unwanted tears pricked at her eyelids. She was unsure if it was fatigue making her weepy or the extreme emotion that she constantly had to hold back whenever she was around him.

His grip tightened on her as he hefted her up a bit. He stopped in the middle of her driveway, directly under the garage light. "Do you really think that I'm worried about neighbors talking, Liz? I'm not. Let me prove it to you."

His lips touched hers, but she only allowed a quick peck.

"Jake, I saw curtains flutter next door. I'm telling you, neighbors are watching!"

He kissed her again, this time like he meant it, and the intensity of it made her feel dizzy. She didn't know how long they kissed, but it left her breathless and wanting more.

Finally she said, "I can walk by myself. Put me down so that you can unlock my door. Besides, how do you think I've been getting around the house the last few days?"

He gave in and set her on her feet, but his hands remained a moment longer than necessary on her hips.

That's when reality started dribbling back into her. As much as she wanted to get to know this man better, it just couldn't happen. Not the way things were for her at the moment. "Night, Jake."

"Good night," he smiled at her.

She stepped into the house and shut the door. "Pleasant dreams," she said to herself while she pressed her back against the door she'd just closed between them.

* * * * *

The next morning, Liz spent a long time in the shower. The warm water washing over her bruises felt good. She wrapped a towel around her head, pulled on her underthings and a housecoat, and slid her feet into her slippers.

She hummed as she moved around the kitchen. Another beautiful sunny day. Footsteps crunched on the gravel walkway next door. She hobbled to the window in time to wave at Jake as he got into his car.

He motioned at the towel on her head and held up one thumb, then laughed and waved.

She posed like a cover girl of old, with one hand behind the towel on her head, and laughed back. Funny that it didn't bother her to be seen like this by Jake.

Her slippers made flip-flopping noises as she walked back into the kitchen and poured water into the coffeepot. She put her finger on the switch to turn the coffee on.

Sparks flew, and a flame shot out.

She screamed, ran to the sink and ran cold water over the electrical burns on two of her fingers.

As the cold water ran over her hand, she looked back at the pot. It was on fire. She grabbed a glass from the cupboard and threw water on it. Since the plastic had melted, coffee ran down the counter and onto the floor.

She'd never heard of a coffeepot doing anything like that before.

It didn't take long to realize the red burn marks were blistering. She immediately went to an aloe plant on the kitchen windowsill, broke off a branch and spread the healing gel onto her fingers. If she was lucky, the aloe might stop the burns from getting worse.

She cleaned up the mess, trying to protect her singed fingers. Every time she looked at the coffeepot, she frowned. How did that happen? And how had water gotten on the floor under her feet before the switch blew? It's a wonder she hadn't been electrocuted.

After she cleaned up the mess in the kitchen, she got out the blow dryer for her hair. She tried to laugh at her silly paranoia, but it didn't stop her from giving the hair dryer a good going-over before she used it.

Finally, dressed in jeans and a blouse, she put on her disguise of sunglasses and the ball cap and hopped into the car. Before she drove off, she checked the contents of her wallet. She still had enough money to do her for a while, but a new coffeepot wasn't exactly a necessity. Being stuck in the house all the time wasn't pleasant, and having a nice hot cup of coffee in the morning was one thing she really enjoyed. She decided she could buy a new coffee maker. It was a luxury she deserved.

Shopping around wasn't on her agenda today, but since she was out, she picked up the Bangor Daily News at the newsstand in the mall, then bought the coffee maker and went straight home. She had to get back to the job of trying to find out what was going on.

Especially since it couldn't be long before someone realized she hadn't died.

With new determination, she worked on the computer all afternoon, stopping only to apply a fresh coat of aloe gel from the plant to her burned fingers. She blessed the plant for its medicinal properties. The aloe and a few other plants had been part of her lease— she'd agree to look after the plants.

She went into the living room and dropped into the recliner, leaned back and put her hands behind her head. She stared at the ceiling, wondering what she could possibly do to find out what was going on. She thought of hiring a detective, but didn't trust anyone enough for that.

Her only lifeline to the world these days had been her few visits with Jake. She'd often watched him leave for work in the mornings while washing breakfast dishes. Just seeing him perked her up more than it should have.

His work hours were irregular and he didn't often arrive home before Ada left. Tonight he didn't return until eleven thirty. She happened to be looking out the window and spotted his car lights from a distance. He pulled into the driveway and got out of his car and strode straight into his house.

He didn't even look at her house to see if she was up! She sighed. In her ideal world he'd come to her door and check on her personally. Good thing she didn't want to get too close to her neighbors.

She crawled into bed, making sure she kept her sore fingers outside of the covers. Things were getting complicated. She cared about Jake, and after the kiss the other night she thought he cared about her. But how would he feel when he found out that everything she'd told him had been a lie, including her name?

The next morning, Liz made sure she was outside having a cup of coffee on the front porch when Jake came out of the house to go to work. The blue dress shirt and dark slacks somehow made his shoulders appear even broader. His brown hair gleamed in the morning light.

At first she didn't think he was going to notice her, but as he leaned over to unlock his car door, his expression changed as he caught sight of her and waved. She waved back, tamping down the thrill of excitement as he crossed the driveway to her. "Morning."

"Morning to you, too. You're looking pretty chipper this morning," she said, catching herself from adding after being out so late. That would definitely have given her away.

Tendrils of still-damp hair curled at the nape of his neck. "Care for a cup of coffee before you go to work?"

He patted his trim midriff. "No, thanks, I'm full of eggs, toast and coffee." He winked and whispered in a conspiratorial tone, "Ada believes in a full breakfast every day. Sometimes, I'd love to have a plain slice of buttered toast, but that would be heresy. Plus, it would hurt her feelings."

"You're just a big teddy bear, aren't you?"

He pulled himself to his full height. "That doesn't sound very manly."

She laughed, set her cup down beside her on the step, and wrapped her arms around her knees, which were drawn up in front of her.

His eyes went to the bruise on her shin. "That's looking quite a bit better, but what's wrong with your fingers?"

She hadn't meant to let him see her fingers. "I burned them when my coffeepot shorted out and caught fire."

He frowned. "Geez, how did that happen?"

"I have no idea," she admitted. "Faulty wiring maybe? Oh well, I'm on the mend now."

"Want to come over tonight?" He looked at his watch.

"Sure, why not?" Even though she should have been running the other way, she had hoped he'd ask.

"Great, I'll call you. Right now I've got to run. Got some work I didn't finish last night, and it's got to be done by ten this morning." He eyed her fingers again and frowned. "See you tonight."

What would she wear? She had very few clothes.

The sun beamed down on her, making her warm and comfortable on her front porch. It was too nice to go in, so she stayed on the porch and enjoyed the fresh air for a while. Little chickadees pecked around the driveway, chirping happily. Their antics kept her amused until Ada came out of Jake's house with a basket of laundry under one arm.

"Morning, Liz," she shouted and waved before walking around the side of the house to the clothesline.

Liz waved. It felt good to smile.

It surprised her when Jake called her about five minutes after he got home. "What time are you coming over?"

"Not yet. You just barely got home."

"I'm just going to have a quick shower, then I thought we could go to town, maybe do a little shopping. You women like that kind of thing, don't you? Then we could catch a show, or go out to eat? What do you think?"

Her insides were in the process of panicking. How in the world would she be able to go out without her disguise? Did she dare go out looking like a normal human being?

This is stupid. I'm in another country. So far, the only scary stranger in her vicinity had been her neighbor and his poodle. "I don't care what we do. You pick." She held her breath. Think, woman. Are you doing the right thing? Her heart said yes, but her head said no.

She looked at her bruises. "Come to think of it, I'm still pretty marked up. I'm a bit of a spectacle. Are you sure this is a good idea?"

"Positive. Be ready at six, okay?"

"Um-hum." She hung up the receiver, looked at her watch. She'd better hurry if she was going to be ready by six. She had to shower, do her hair and iron her one and only dress. Little butterflies tumbled around inside her chest, and she felt like a teenager going on a first date.

Chapter Five

Jake hung up the phone and went to the kitchen.

Ada put the dishtowel on the rack to dry and ran her hands over her ample hips. "By the way, what were you doing next door at Liz's house this morning?" She grinned knowingly at him. "I wasn't wrong about that one, was I? You like her, don't you?"

"She's a nice lady," he said.

"She's a jumpy one, though, isn't she?"

He nodded, pushing away fears that Liz might be in more trouble than he knew. At the same time, he wanted to help.

Meanwhile, Ada's expression deflated. She'd obviously hoped for more interesting news.

She'd make it a big deal if he told her about his date tonight, a date that meant nothing other than Liz needing to get out of the house. And there was no reason they couldn't go out as friends. He had to admit he was a little worried about taking her out, though. She seemed to have a fear of being out in public. He wondered if she had one of those phobias, cabin fever or something? Then again, if she were hiding from a husband, she wouldn't want to be seen, either.

Maybe he'd be able to coax some tangible information from her tonight. Was she hiding out? And from whom?

Shortly after Ada left for the day, he walked over to Liz's place and rang the bell. The door opened almost immediately.

Her soft perfume greeted his nostrils, and she looked fantastic in a purple sundress that accentuated her body in the most amazing ways. She had her hair done up in a bun at the back and had applied a little makeup so she didn't look as pale. He preferred her hair loose and wondered why women felt they had to restrict their lovely locks when they dressed up.

He wasn't the least bit surprised that she looked nervous, though he wished he had even the slightest inkling about her problem. "Smile, we're going to have fun," he said.

"Sure we are." Though her words sounded bright, they didn't quite gain the level of believability she'd probably aimed for. Her eyes told the whole truth, even though she didn't seem to be aware of giving herself away. She was afraid.

He opened the car door for her. As he walked around to his side, she stared straight ahead and kept still as a statue while he started the engine and backed out of the driveway. Her face had gone from fearful to completely pale, her hands clenched in her lap.

"Dinner first?" he asked, trying to add happiness to his tone as he glanced sideways at her white complexion. What darkness or horror kept her lovely face from showing him the beauty that lurked behind her smile?

"Sounds wonderful." Even though she forced a smile, no joy reached her eyes.

"Are you sure you want to do this?"

Liz gazed out her car window. They left their street and headed uptown. "Of course."

She smiled again.

This time he could tell she was trying much harder to appear happy, but he still didn't buy her act.

In the restaurant, Liz picked at her food and kept glancing around the room like she expected to see someone she didn't want to see. His spirits deflated. It had to be a husband or former boyfriend. What else could it be?

Jake took a big bite of lasagna. Should he ask her about an ex? If he forced her to tell the truth, would he scare her off? He really didn't want to ruin their evening, though it was evident that Liz wasn't enjoying herself.

He paid the check, and they strode to his car.

"I have a bit of a headache," she said.

No surprise, she'd been so tense. "I have Tylenol at home, if you still need it when we get there. If not, I have a great bottle of wine we can share."

She frowned, but at least she didn't say no.

"No strings attached, just a glass of wine and a relaxing evening. What do you think?" He had every intention of plying her with alcohol, then trying to get her to talk. Not fair maybe. But necessary.

He could see a difference in her demeanor as soon as they returned to the privacy of his home. That taut, fearful expression had vanished, and her smile once again brightened.

She didn't ask for anything for her headache, so he handed her a glass of wine.

"Thanks." She took a sip and wandered into the living room. He followed, turned on some music, making sure the melody was low enough it wouldn't interrupt their conversation.

He sat down on the chair opposite her on the couch. "To Liz and to all enigmas." He held up his glass in a toast.

She frowned slightly, but raised her glass and took a sip. "Enigma, huh? I'd prefer to call myself realistic with a hint of mystery."

"Okay. Tell me a bit about your mysterious self." He pretended that he didn't notice the alarmed look that crossed her face.

"Not much to tell," she said.

"Married?" he asked, when it was obvious that she wasn't about to share any truths with him.

"No!"

She was extremely quick to shout that out. Too quick?

"Divorced?"

"No, why are you asking me that?"

He offered to refill her glass, but she put her hand over the top. "No, thanks. One is enough."

"I'm sorry, I didn't mean to be intrusive. It's just that something seems to be bothering you. You're nervous, almost afraid. I'd like to help, if I can." Yeah, he'd lost his freaking mind. He just couldn't stop himself from trying to help.

She looked down at her empty wine glass before setting it on the coffee table. "I think we'd better call it a night. Thanks for dinner. And I really do appreciate you worrying about me, but it's not at all necessary. I'm just an average person. There's no reason for you to feel that you have to help me." Her words sounded strained.

"But..."

"Good night, Jake."

Before he could come up with a good enough response, she'd slammed out of his house. Damn!

* * * * *

Liz let herself into her rental home and slammed the door behind her. She jammed all the locks securely into place, turned on all of the lights, and wandered from room to room, doing a safety check. She hated this! She hated not trusting anyone and having to do everything alone. Especially when Jake so obviously wanted to help. He had no idea how deeply she wished she could trust him.

Later, she donned her pajamas and crawled into bed. Tears of frustration threatened.

Sure, he might want to scare away a mean ex-husband, but what would his reaction be to having to scare away an assailant who'd possibly killed her parents and blown up her home while trying to kill her, too?

Even though she slept fitfully that night, the next morning didn't seem as dismal. Yes, she'd had a few accidents, but she shouldn't blow everything out of proportion. Whoever had attacked her in Maine hadn't found her. She was safe here.

While drinking her morning coffee, she glanced at the computer. She'd forgotten to turn it off last night. A message flashed across the screen. Strange. She crossed to the computer and read the message. You Have Mail.

How could she possibly have mail? No one knew her e-mail address.

She reached out to open the mailbox but stopped herself. This was silly. Some company had deposited a cookie on her hard drive during one of her Internet searches in order to send her a commercial message. Yes, of course. That had to be it.

She tapped her finger on her lip, reached out again to click the button then stopped. Maybe she'd have breakfast first. Instant Breakfast would be nice.

She'd put it on the second shelf from the top, behind the cereal. Her hand had barely rested on the first shelf while she reached into the cupboard when the shelving collapsed. Cans flew out at her like missiles before she could get out of the way.

One can hit her forehead. Pain blossomed, and she saw stars for a second. Another can slammed into her foot. She fell backward onto the floor and rolled out of the way while the rest of the shelves seemed to implode and collapse in reaction to the first shelf going. Everything flew out. Except for the can hitting her head and foot, she'd been extremely lucky.

Geez, her head stung like the devil. She could feel a nasty lump rising, and it hurt to touch. If she kept going like this, she'd have to fill the freezer in the basement with bags of ice or frozen peas.

That reminded her of the episode in the basement. She winced. She hadn't gone down those stairs since she'd fallen. Okay, what was going on? Could cupboards fall apart on their own? Three incidents in a week?

She was beginning to see the light of day, and she didn't like the view.

Pushing herself up off the floor, she carefully prodded the rising lump on her forehead then surveyed the wreckage around her. Cans and boxes littered the floor. It looked like a scrapyard.

The enormity of her situation struck her.

She went to the hall, picked up the phone and dialed the landlord. It was time to find out if this place needed to be condemned.

He came right over.

His expression the moment he stepped inside the door worried her. He thought she'd done this.

"I didn't order any oil for that tank, Ms. Davidson," he stated coldly, giving her the strangest look. He looked at her forehead. "Are you all right? Want me to call you a doctor or something?"

"No, I want you to explain these accidents that have happened to me lately." She stood at the opening of the basement stairs, while he checked the pipe with a flashlight. "It beats the hell out of me how this little round hole got in the pipe. It isn't even in a seam. And regardless of the hole, where'd the oil come from? I don't put oil in these tanks until September or October. If that oil company is trying to get money out of me at this time of the year, I'll have their hides!"

He looked at the newest lump on her head and frowned. "You say you fell down the stairs a few days ago?"

She was sure he noted the rest of her bruises were older and starting to turn yellow.

"My coffeepot also shorted out and burned my fingers." She showed him the red marks from the burns. "And this morning, I opened the cupboard and all of the shelves inside collapsed. I got hit in the head with a can."

He turned white and looked like he might pass out. "Hey, what's going on here? Is this a scam to get insurance money?"

"What? No. Of course not," she said. "If I were going to sue you, don't you think I would have done it after I fell down the stairs?"

"Maybe. Maybe not." His voice got cooler by the minute.

"I want you to check the cupboards," she said.

They entered the kitchen, and he gasped and started yelling at her. "I'll tell you one thing, little lady. I don't think you'll be getting your damage deposit back. Look at my cupboards." He stepped carefully over broken dishes and cans and looked into the cupboard. "Hand me that flashlight."

She handed it to him, reining back a caustic comment. She needed him on her side. Suddenly, nausea announced itself in undulating waves. Realizing the bump on her head must be the cause, she climbed over broken dishes and canned goods to sit down at the kitchen table.

She put her head down on the table to offset a wave of dizziness.

"What the…" He shoved aside some broken glass and climbed up onto the counter top on his knees and stuck his head right into the cupboard along with the flashlight. He jumped back down and turned to face her with his hands on his hips. "No more foolin' around, lady¬. These shelves were cut!"

She raised her aching head from the table and gaped at him. "Cut? With what?"

"Don't play dumb with me. These shelves were cut with a saw of some kind. Why would you do these things to yourself for a bit of my insurance money? I don't have much, I tell you. You'll be sorry that you put yourself through all this pain, because you're not getting a red cent out of me."

"I didn't do this!" she said.

"Then who the hell did?" He'd been such a nice man when they first met. But now his eyes were bulging, and his skin mottled. He looked like he might pass out himself.

She swallowed. Yes, the question now would definitely be...who the hell did? The room started to spin again. She felt herself falling, and everything went black.

"Liz?" Something cold touched the back of her neck. She moaned and opened her eyes. She didn't feel like she was on the floor anymore, but rather on something soft and comfortable.

"Liz, wake up."

Her eyes focused suddenly. "Jake! What are you doing here?" She looked around. How had she gotten to her bedroom? Jake had a cold, wet towel against the lump on her forehead. She pulled the bag of ice out from behind her neck.

"The landlord came and got me. He was going to call an ambulance and the police, but I wouldn't let him."

"Why didn't he phone the cops from here?" she asked. Why'd he go to Jake's place? Her suspicions were getting the best of her now.

"Your phone is out," he said. "Doesn't rain, but it pours, I guess."

No, there was a much more sinister reason behind all of her troubles. Her assailant had found her.

"I would have called the ambulance myself, if you hadn't been all right. But I figured you wouldn't want an ambulance. Was I right?" His expression was fraught with tension.

"Yes, that's right. No ambulance."

"Just know if you get any worse from that bang on your head, I'm still going to call them, no matter what you say." He cradled her hand in his own. She lifted her head and looked around the room. The landlord stood behind him, wringing his hands in her bedroom doorway. Sweat glistened on his irate-looking face.

"Look, Jake," he blurted out, "if this is a scam, it's not going to work. I'm retired. You know I don't have the kind of money that would cover a lawsuit."

"Calm down, George," Jake soothed the aged landlord. "Liz isn't like that. I don't know what's going on, but I can tell you that this wasn't something she did to herself."

"I'm going home now, Jake. You tell missy I'll call the carpenters to fix up the mess, but she's paying for the work. I'm not paying to fix cupboards that were deliberately sawed in two." He pointed his gnarled old finger at her. "And she poked a hole in my oil pipe, she did. Would've taken some doing, that. It's a heavy pipe, not easy to put a hole in."

Jake nodded in agreement. "I'll tell her George."

The landlord stomped out of the room and down the stairs, still mumbling to himself.

Liz felt as if she'd been holding her breath until the angry man left her alone with Jake. He sat down next to her on the bed.

"What's going on, Liz?" he asked.

"Someone's trying to kill me." She swallowed and closed her eyes. She hadn't planned on telling him the whole truth. But the way things were going, she didn't have a choice. She couldn't bluff her way out of this one. "I thought I was safe, but he must've followed me here."

His expression changed from stunned to incredulous. She had really hoped somehow that he would instinctively believe her. But in her heart she knew believing the truth would be a stretch for anyone.

"Who is trying to kill you?" he asked calmly, almost patronizingly, while a new light of understanding filled his expression. Only she didn't think she'd like what he was thinking.

"I don't know." She considered telling him the whole sordid story, but she was tired now. She'd tell him later. "Can we at least wait until my headache goes away?"

"Sure," he said.

He spent the day with her. Getting her tea, cleaning up the mess in the kitchen and keeping her off her feet. And he didn't ask any questions. She blessed him for that. By nighttime, she felt like she might live. At least the worst of the headache had gone away, thanks to acetaminophen every four hours.

She'd moved to the living room and tried to watch a little television rather than having him climb the stairs to her bedroom every half hour. She yawned and regretted stretching her arms. She hurt all over.

"You should go to bed," he said, sitting across from her in the living room after dark had fallen.

"I can't thank you enough for your help today."

"Do you want to talk about this afternoon?" he asked, leaning back and waiting for an explanation.

She wasn't ready. She had to be sure first that it was the right thing to do. "There's not much to tell. Whoever lived here before must've tried to fix the cupboards and forgot to reattach that shelf properly."

"Liz, the wood has been cut with a saw."

"Yeah, but it must've been the people who used to live—"

"It's a fresh cut."

"Oh." That meant the person who wanted her dead had really found her. "I can't explain it," she said, but her words faded away and her insides turned acidic. Her nerve endings reacted and throbbed in unison with her stomachache.

"You said someone was trying to kill you." His strained expression made a knot form in her chest.

"Did I? I don't remember."

"Is it true?"

"No," she said. Liar, liar, pants on fire!

Worse. He didn't even try to hide the fact that he didn't believe her. "You look like hell," he said. "Go to sleep, okay? I'll wake you up once in a while to make sure you're okay."

She shook her head then regretted the motion. Maybe he had a point. It felt as if she had a metal ball bulging inside the frontal area of her skull. "Would you mind getting me some water and more painkillers first?"

"Sure."

She didn't like this quiet, suspicious version of the Jake she knew. She wanted him to laugh and joke with her. He wouldn't be doing that anymore. She could tell he thought she was a psycho.

True to his word, he woke her up off and on throughout the night. He must've slept on the couch.

The next morning she pushed off the sheet and slowly opened her eyes while her fingers gingerly tested her forehead. The lump remained, but she felt somewhat better. She eased her way into the bathroom and eyed herself in the mirror. "You gorgeous thing you," she said aloud as she looked at her bruised forehead and puffy eyes.

Bending over to pick up her housecoat made her forehead feel like it might crack wide open. Then she slowly shuffled downstairs to the kitchen, trying not to jar her head with her footsteps.

The kitchen had been cleaned up. Cans that had been all over the floor had been stacked on the counter. She saw that only a single cup and a small plate had been spared. Jake must've thrown the rest of the shards out. The cupboard shelves still hung in broken bits.

She looked around and saw her new coffeepot had miraculously survived the avalanche of dishes and cans. If nothing else, she could have a cup of coffee this morning.

"Morning," he said.

She screamed and spun around, then grabbed her head.

Jake held up both hands. "Oh man, I'm sorry. I thought you knew I stayed all night."

"I don't think I'm able to even think straight right now." She steadied herself against the table.

A persistent dull thud inside her skull made her feel fuzzy enough, but seeing him standing there did stranger things to her equilibrium.

"Let's get you a cup of coffee, and you can tell me what the devil is going on," he said. Apparently, he'd given up waiting until she felt better.

They sat at the table looking at each other for a minute before she broke eye contact and looked away. She could see the fresh cuts on the wooden shelves from here, and that scared her all over again. She had a decision to make today. Stay or run again.

"I might as well tell you the truth, Jake. Someone is trying to kill me, and I believe the same person killed my parents." She glanced across the kitchen at the still-flashing cursor on her computer. It reminded her that she'd received mail the day before. "All I can tell you is that I'm in danger, apparently even inside this house! I have no idea why."

She got up slowly and crossed to the computer and clicked on her mailbox.

The message that opened on her screen made her blood run cold.

I may have missed you in Bangor. But I'll get you when you least suspect it.

She gasped and looked at Jake, who'd read the message over her shoulder.

"See? It's a message from whoever is after me!" She could manage only a whisper, because her throat was threatening to close off. "There's your proof."

"Who is it from?" he asked, leaning over her and moving the mouse to find out who the e-mail came from. They both gasped at the same time.

This isn't happening, Liz thought, closing her eyes. Her breath felt like it was trapped inside a balloon in her chest.

"It came from you. You sent it to yourself," he said slowly.

Suddenly, the room turned cold. Her mouth opened and closed, but nothing came out. The thought that someone had been in her house long enough to use her computer couldn't be true. If this was a new tactic, rather than blowing her up, it just might work, because now it looked like she was some kind of a nut trying to make people think someone was trying to kill her when it appeared she was really trying to hurt herself.

Jake's expression was worse than pity. It was distrust. He believed she'd sent the message to herself.

"Jake, I didn't send that message. Don't you see? Whoever sent this e-mail has been in my house. That's how all of those accidents happened to me. Whoever he is, he's trying very hard to make it look like an accident. I don't know why. Can't you believe me?"

His silence said it all.

Turning her head, she looked at the message on the computer again. The realization of the depth of cunning that had gone into making her look like she was crazy hit her. "The e-mail can't help me, can it? This person has outsmarted me by using my own computer and e-mail account to send the message."

"Unless they left fingerprints."

A spark of hope shot through her. Did he believe her after all? Or did he think she was delusional and that they would find her own fingerprints?

"Whoever is doing this is too smart for that." She racked her brain, trying to think of anything that could prove she was telling the truth.

She made up her mind. She told Jake the whole story about the deaths of her parents and the vandalism that had led up to the house explosion. She felt drained by having to repeat what she'd been through over the last few months, but she also felt a sense of relief. She'd shared it with someone else. Maybe that allowed her some emotional release.

"The killer nearly got me, but I got away and thought I might be safe if I left the country. I'm obviously not safe anywhere."

"You seem to have a problem," he said in a monotone.

"Of course I have a problem! Someone is trying to kill me!"

He exhaled. "Liz…all of your accidents and the message to yourself…it looks bad." He shuffled his feet and looked down. "Are you sure you don't know who's doing this?"

"You're not serious." Her eyes implored him.

His look of disbelief reminded her of the police in Bangor. For a moment, she'd dared to believe in him, but he obviously didn't believe her and might even think she had a mental illness.

"I'm telling you that someone is trying to kill me. That's why I moved here—to try to get away. I've wanted to tell you the truth, but was afraid you wouldn't believe me. Obviously, I was right."

"I'm sorry." His gaze went to her computer again.

"I didn't send that message to myself!" Heat burned at the backs of her eyes. There would be no help for her. She was alone in the world. Even Jake didn't believe her—but then why would he?

She sat straighter. Made a decision. "Please leave." She should've paid attention to her intuition. She should've known better than to let someone into her life.

"I want to help you, Liz, if you'll let me."

"How? You don't believe me. And I have no idea who wants me dead. I can tell you one thing, whoever it is, they're very proficient at making it look like an accident every time something happens to me."

"You're sure this is real? I mean, do you think you could be subconsciously getting hurt without realizing it?"

She narrowed her gaze on him. Why hadn't he left already? She'd told him to leave. "What exactly are you saying?"

"Is there a chance you're having blackouts or some sort of seizures and don't know it?"

"You need to go," she said in a low, angry voice.

He left but obviously didn't want to. She slammed the door shut and winced when the sounded reverberated in her head. She returned to the kitchen.

If her assailant had deliberately tried to make her look crazy, he'd succeeded. And if it was just pure luck that it had happened this way, he must be quite tickled with the turn of events. If he couldn't kill her by making it look like an accident, she feared now that he'd make her look suicidal. He could then kill her any old way he wanted. All he'd have to do would be leave a suicide note.

Should she run again? But what good would that do? He'd found her too quickly. How did he know she hadn't died in the explosion? Especially when the media were still reporting her as being dead.

Feeling desolate and almost unafraid, because she was nearly at the point of giving up, she needed to get out of this place for a bit. She was no safer at home than outside, anyway. She limped to the car because her toe hurt as well as her shin. Her face looked like she'd been in a boxing match, and later, when she bought lunch at a small bistro, the waitress eyed her critically, probably because the ball cap and sunglasses didn't quite hide her bruises. Better to let people think some crazy husband had beaten her than to try to convince anyone of the truth, a truth that made no sense to her, let alone anyone else.

Still considering whether she should run again or stay put, she decided to at least spend one more night. No way could she pack up and travel while her head still throbbed and she was a little dizzy off and on.

When she got home, she checked the house from the freaky basement to the upstairs. She even pulled down the ladder and climbed up into the attic. Being scared to the point of insanity pushed her beyond fear. All appeared to be clear. Now, with the doors locked and a chair jammed under the basement doorknob, she crawled into bed. Sleep didn't come easily, and by the time the sun filtered in through her window, she'd resolved a few of her problems. Number one being, if she wanted to live, she had to fight back. She stuck her banged-up leg out from under the covers and looked at it. Her bruises were turning a putrid yellow, but her shin felt better today.

Her head still hurt, but all her aches and pains were lessening.

After a steamy, hot shower, she pulled on a pair of jeans and a lightweight sweatshirt, ate breakfast and donned her usual disguise—ball cap and sunglasses. One last run for supplies and she'd consider making a run for it. As soon as she could figure out where to go, that is.

Something bright flashed from across the street as she neared her car. What was it? She looked at the street. No vehicles. The neighbor's house looked uninhabited, as it usually did during the day.

She got into the car and drove away from the house. She liked feeling more in control of her fear.

Either way, she couldn't afford to rent another house. She'd sunk too much money into this place. It crossed her mind she should just go home to Maine and let the police know she was alive. At least that way she'd have access to her bank account again.

The flash of light niggled at her. She turned onto Regent Street and started up the hill. Wait! That flash of sunlight might have reflected off something pointed at her. Binoculars or a rifle!

No, it couldn't be a rifle scope. She couldn't commit suicide by shooting herself from far away. On the other hand, her attacker might have tired of playing cat and mouse.

She didn't blame Jake for having doubts about her. The way things had been so insidiously choreographed, it was a wonder she believed it herself. Darn it, one little flash of light and the debilitating fear threatened to boil to the surface again.

By the time she returned home, it was almost noon. The sun's rays felt extremely soothing, and the temperature had soared into the eighties. She parked the car and stepped out, looking nervously around. She scanned the bushes across the street where the flash of light might have initiated. She hadn't really seen where for sure. Short of going over and checking the bushes, which she wasn't going to do, she couldn't see anything.

A small drop of perspiration trickled from under her hat and slid down her face. Time to get into cooler clothes. After unlocking the front door, she listened inside until she felt she was safe to enter. She made a quick check of the house, but avoided the basement and attic this time. Besides, the chair was still propped under the knob of the basement door, and she had placed a string in the opening of the attic door. Neither had been dislodged. She went to her bedroom, stripped off her jeans and long-sleeved shirt and reached for her shorts and tank top, which she had folded and put on top of her dresser the day before. The clothes were gone.

She glanced around. Had she put them somewhere else and forgotten?

Shivers rode her spine. Her clothes lay neatly piled on the trunk at the bottom of her bed. Had she done that?

No way. And her personal things looked just slightly out of place. Her bra was inside out. She was anal about folding her bras right-side out.

Steeling against the coiling serpent of fear in her stomach and against the thought that her attacker might be in the house right now, she forced herself to seem unaware that someone might be watching her. Panicking right now might tip him off that she knew he'd been in her room, that he might be hiding in her closet. She had to pretend she was oblivious, but her insides were jiggling and ready to explode with panic.

Still standing in the center of her room in her bra and panties, she quickly snatched her shorts and yanked them on, willing herself not to panic.

She scanned the room. Her breathing sounded erratic even to her. If he was hiding in her closet, she wanted him to believe she had no idea he was there.

The closet door was shut.

Had she shut it before she left? She couldn't remember.

She stepped into the hallway with pinpricks of electricity zinging along her arms and legs. She dashed down the stairs toward the front door as if her life depended on it. Forget pretending to be oblivious.

Making it to the bottom of the stairs, she snagged her purse off the hall table and ripped open the front door. The sound of it slamming behind her was music to her ears.

No one followed.

Feeling a little more secure outside the house, she hoped she'd been wrong. Maybe she had moved the clothes herself. She'd taken a hard knock to the head, after all. Had she developed a memory problem?

She looked back at the house. She hadn't locked it. Should she go back?

No frigging way!

What difference did locking the door make anyway? Her assailant seemed to come and go at will. She shivered at the thought.

She scurried across the driveway, forcing her tight muscles to move.

Jake wouldn't be home right now, but Ada would be. Liz could make up a reason to stay until he got home. No way would she go back to that house alone. Not even to grab her stuff to leave.

Jake didn't believe her, but for her own peace of mind, she needed him to. She'd come to the decision that it mattered what he thought, and she wanted to prove to him that she wasn't crazy.

Panic still licked at her heels until she reached the kitchen door. Knock. Knock. Harder this time. Where was Ada?

Keep your cool, girl. She slanted a glance back at her rental house. Had the curtains moved in her bedroom?

Finally, Ada opened the door with a surprised look on her face, and Liz practically pushed her way inside.

"Liz, I haven't seen you for a while, dear. Come right in."

Moot point, since she was already in. If she noticed Liz's distress, she didn't mention it.

Ada shut the door, and Liz resisted the urge to lock it. Besides, it appeared her assailant wanted her demise to look like an accident. She didn't think he'd come barging into Jake's house, not with another person here—hopefully.

"Have a seat at the kitchen table, dear," Ada said. "I'll be done here in a minute, then I'll make us a cup of tea." She went back to kneading bread and chatting happily.

"Jake is lucky to have someone like you taking care of him, Ada." Liz tried to sound normal, but to her own ears she sounded winded, terrified.

"Thank you, dear." Ada kneaded the bread a few more times. "Let's have a cup of tea when I'm done."

"May I put the kettle on for you? Your hands are covered with flour," Liz said.

"Lovely," Ada said, indicating the kettle with a doughy finger. "What brings you over? Just visiting?" Flour motes floated in the air while she attacked the dough again, making Ada rub her nose with her forearm. "Or were you just lonely?"

"Lonely," Liz said, happy to grasp at the choice, then had a brilliant idea to stay here for the day. "And the landlord has someone doing a bit of pesticide spraying in the house. So I have to stay out for a while." She hated lying to the woman. She'd never lied before these attacks started happening to her, and this little white lie stuck in her throat like a dry wad of bread.

"Oh, that explains it then," Ada said.

"Explains what?"

"The man I saw around your place this morning. He was at the side of the house earlier, and I was just about to call the police. I knew you weren't home because your car was gone. But then he disappeared, so I assumed he left. He must have been the exterminator."

Liz's heart pounded so hard it felt like her ribs might crack under the pressure. "What did he look like?" she asked, trying to keep her voice casual. Would there be a chance that she might find out?

"He was in the shadows of the elm trees between our houses. I didn't really get a very good look." Ada frowned at her. "Heavy set though and wearing a ball cap."

Liz turned her face away and concentrated on pouring water into the kettle and turning it on. She took her time, trying to compose herself before she sat at the kitchen table again. The sound of bread being kneaded faded away while she tried to fathom what she should do about being found by her attacker again. If she got Ada to tell Jake about seeing the man, it could prove someone had been around her house. But Ada hadn't gotten a good look. It might've been the next-door neighbor with his poodle again, for all Ada knew. But Liz knew better.

Ada gave the bread one last pat then put it into a bowl and covered it with a damp cloth.

To stay sane, Liz made small talk, to try to force the terrors of her reality into a section of her brain where she couldn't grasp it for a few seconds. "I can't make bread, but my mother taught me how to make piecrust." As soon as the words were out of her mouth, she knew she'd made a mistake. She'd left herself open to questions about her mother.

"Where does your mother live, dear?"

"She died last year." Liz looked at her clasped hands on the tabletop, then looked out the window. A direct line to her house.

"Oh, I'm so sorry, Liz."

The kettle began to whistle. Liz started to get up, but Ada beat her to it. She rinsed her hands under the tap and got the cups out of the cupboard. "Let me make you a nice cup of tea."

"I hope I'm not keeping you from anything, Ada. Maybe I could help you with your chores? Make your day go a little faster?"

Ada raised one eyebrow. "By the look of you, my dear, I don't exactly think you're in any shape to work today. Where'd you get all of those bruises?"

Dressed in shorts and a short-sleeved T-shirt, Liz had forgotten about how she looked. "Oh, I slipped and fell down a couple of stairs a few days ago. It's nothing. The bruises look worse than they are."

Liz took a sip of the tea that Ada had given her.

"My goodness, you're shaking." Ada reached out and patted her hand. "Did you get a whiff of those pesticides when you shouldn't have?"

"Possibly. I forgot I was supposed to stay out of there for a while," she lied again and hated herself for it.

Chapter Six

Jake had been too busy to check on Liz during the day. He'd intended to but had been mired in an incoming storm front and had had to quickly prepare the models.

By the time he got home and pulled into the driveway, the sun was setting. It surprised him to see Ada's car still there. She didn't usually stay late, especially on bingo nights. Something must be up, because she went to bingo faithfully.

When he stepped inside, Ada met him at the door.

"Hello. I'm surprised you are you still here? What's up?" It was then that he saw Liz curled up and sleeping on the window seat.

Ada pressed one finger over her lips. "Shhh. She got a whiff of pesticides at her house today. Evidently, the landlord did some spraying there, and Liz forgot about it and went inside. She hasn't been feeling very well all afternoon." Ada put down the paper she'd been reading at the kitchen table. "I think she must have gotten quite a big jolt of pesticides. She was acting kind of nervous and strange this afternoon. Finally, her eyes got heavy, and she curled up on the window seat and fell asleep." Ada looked at Liz and shook her head and clucked. "Poor thing. She's all tuckered out."

Jake allowed his gaze to linger on Liz. Sun filtered through the curtains and across her striking facial features.

He frowned. What was he going to do about her? Did she have delusions or was she telling the truth about someone wanting her dead? The whole idea just seemed too far-fetched, and even though he wanted to believe her, he didn't know if he could.

"I'm off for home," Ada whispered, throwing her unnecessary sweater over her arm. "Why don't you let her sleep awhile? She just fell asleep a short time ago."

"I'll do that, Ada," he whispered back.

"Night, sweetie. Oh, and your supper's in the fridge. Actually, I put up two plates, just in case." She looked at Liz again. "I made chicken cordon bleu, fiddleheads and Caesar salad. And, of course, my homemade bread."

"That sounds great. Good luck at bingo tonight. I'll see you tomorrow."

He glanced down at Liz after Ada left. He should trust this pale woman. For some strange reason, he had a feeling she wouldn't lie to him. He inhaled a ragged breath.

His gut churned, but he tore himself away to wash up before dinner.

He cut his face three times while shaving. Oh hell, he might as well admit to himself that he believed her. She just didn't come across as someone who hurt herself for attention. He sighed. His gut sense was usually correct about people, and he had the feeling it was correct this time, too.

Maybe he could take a risk on her. Maybe all she needed was someone to believe in her. He sure as hell needed to believe in himself again. Trust his instincts.

Twenty minutes later, he stepped out of the shower, towelled himself off and crossed the hallway, wrapped in a towel. Running his fingers through damp hair, he entered his bedroom and approached the dresser. He caught sight of her in the mirror, sitting on the edge of his bed.

"Liz?"

She didn't seem at all flustered at his lack clothing. He also noted she spent some time checking him out. "What are you doing in here?"

"I woke up alone and felt a little nervous. I heard the shower running, so I came up here to wait for you." She swallowed and looked the other way. "I guess I didn't think this through." A blush had crept up her neck to her face.

He rechecked the closure of his towel.

"I'll wait in the hallway while you get dressed. But don't be long, okay?" She hesitantly got up and strode across the room, stopping at the doorway.

He watched her go, hair slightly tousled from her sleep, cheeks flushed from the sun shining on her—or seeing him in only a towel—her lips glossy and wanting to be kissed. Damn, that's the last thing she needed from him.

When she shut the door between them, he yanked on a pair of shorts and a T-shirt with lightning speed. He looked at himself in the mirror, ran the brush through his wet hair, took a deep breath and crossed to the door.

The fact that she was still outside his bedroom door said it all. Something more had really spooked her.

"What's going on? Ada mentioned pesticides? Why was your house being fumigated?" He sighed, fighting a dreadful fear that she might be on the rim of a very dangerous precipice. Could he stop her from going over the edge?

"It wasn't really pesticides." She looked repentant and followed him to the stairs. "I hated to lie to Ada, but there was a strange man skulking around my place today. I think he was inside," she hissed. "My clothes were moved around, and I was in the middle of the room in my underwear when I realized that the closet door was closed and I might not have closed it."

He gritted his teeth. How should he handle this?

"Don't you see? He might have been inside," she said, putting her hand on her throat.

"Inside your closet?" he asked.

"Yes." She gave him a funny look. "You believe me, don't you?"

"Let's try to figure this out first. Let's go downstairs and have something to drink." He urged her down the hallway, hating himself for being attracted to her right now. She needed his help.

And how could he help if his hormones blinded him to the fact that she had a problem—one way or another? He got her a tall glass of ice water. "Look, we'll talk about this. But we should eat first. Ada left supper for us." He moved to the fridge and removed their dinner plates, which were still warm. They just needed a couple of minutes in the microwave.

Liz seemed less stressed now.

"So you think someone has been in your place again?" At this point he would do almost anything to take away that tired, frightened look she wore almost constantly.

"Yes, I'm positive." She rubbed her arms and looked at the floor. "And Jake?"

"Yes?"

"This time Ada saw him. He exists."

His heartbeat picked up. Proof! Yes, he needed a little bit of that right now. "Good," he said. "Where did she see him?"

"Lurking around the garage this morning while I was out. She assumed he was the exterminator since I told her the place had been fumigated. I didn't want to tell her about my troubles. It's bad enough I told you."

"I'm glad you told me. And it's really good that someone else saw him." Note to self: Call Ada later and ask her about it. He wanted to know for sure that Ada had seen this man and ask her what the hell he looked like.

"As far as I know, Ada is the only one who's seen him. I certainly haven't." She paced to the kitchen window and glance furtively toward her house through the curtains. She needed a cop, not a meteorologist. Hell, she needed a bodyguard. "Ada didn't get a good look, though. He was heavy-set with a cap. Could've been anybody."

"Could've been your next-door neighbor with the poodle." Jake set their warmed plates on the table and poured a couple glasses of ice water then sat opposite her.

"Eat first, then we'll talk. I don't know about you, but I'm famished."

She ate every bite, then smiled at him. Why'd she have to look at him like that? He took a big gulp of ice water.

"Dessert?"

"No, thank you."

"Let's go into the living room and talk this whole thing over now."

"Why don't I do the dishes while we talk?"

"Never mind those," he said. "I'll do them later. Right now we need to talk about this man Ada saw." He took her hand and pulled her toward the living room. "Have you considered it might have been someone hired by your landlord? Maybe he was just fixing something up around the house?"

Her eyes began to water immediately. "Why can't you believe me, Jake? I'm not asking you to vanquish my demons. How can you? I don't even know who they are. All I want is for you to believe in me. I'm alone, with no one to even care if I'm killed. I just need to know that if this evil monster gets his way, someone will make sure he comes to justice." She blinked and looked away. "I realize no matter how much I try, I might not be so lucky the next time. He's insidious, slinking into my home when I'm not around and leaving traps for me." She touched the sore spot on her forehead as if to remind herself.

Jake rubbed at the furrows between his brows.

"If I could face him, I'd fight back. At least then I'd have the dignity of knowing that I stood up for myself. I'm not a coward. At least I don't think I am." She looked away, then mumbled, "I hope I won't be when the time comes."

He reached out to her but pulled back as she shrank away from his hand.

She didn't want his pity, and he had the feeling it took everything she had not to burst into tears right now. Any amount of sympathy might open the dreaded floodgates, and she'd been trying too hard to prove she was tough.

"What are you thinking?" she asked.

He shook his head and ran his fingers through his hair, creating furrows through the thick, slightly damp mass. "I want to believe you. I honestly do." He looked directly at her.

"But?" Her expression demanded that he tell her the truth.

"I need time to figure this whole thing out." His heart squeezed at the raw pain etched into her beautiful face.

"Jake, I don't blame you for thinking there's something wrong with me. I've been over it the last few days, and if these things were happening to someone else, I'm not sure I'd believe them either." She looked past him at a spot on the ceiling. "I realize, too, that you've been more caring and kind than most people would be under the circumstances. No matter what happens, I really appreciate everything you've done for me."

"Liz , I..."

She held up a hand. "Don't say anything. It isn't necessary. And you don't have to believe me. It's enough that you helped me even when you're not sure what's going on. What more could I ask?"

He looked down at his feet.

She held a hand over her mouth as she tried to stifle a yawn.

"You're tired. I'll walk you home?" That familiar shadow of fear crossed her face. She couldn't hide it, no matter how hard she tried. "Do you want to stay here tonight?"

"No, but thank you anyway. Would you mind walking me home, though, and maybe taking a quick look around inside?"

He got off the couch. "I'll just be a minute." He ran up the stairs two at a time and got his overnight bag. She needed help even though she wouldn't ask for it. He'd sleep on her couch tonight and let her get a decent night's sleep. He grabbed his laptop, too. He'd start doing some research while he was at it. Maybe he could find something to give some credence to her fears.

Chapter Seven

When he came back downstairs, he held a bag in his hand. "Where are you going?" she asked.

"If you won't stay here tonight, then I'm going to stay at your place."

She opened her mouth to tell him no, but said, "Thank you." She needed human contact. She felt lonely and missed her family.

The worst part was that things had been so out of control lately, she'd barely had time to miss her parents. Remorse stabbed her when she realized she'd been able to forget her beloved parents for days at a time. She rubbed her eyes with her fists, her vision blurred. Too often lately, mind-numbing fatigue cut into her clarity.

"You need a good night's sleep. You're exhausted. And if I'm on the couch, you won't have to worry because I won't let anything happen to you."

"I don't know," she said.

"It's no big deal. Things will look so much better if you get a dozen hours of sleep."

"I have to admit, I've been sleeping pretty poorly for the last few days."

"It's settled, then. Let's go." He held the door open for her. She instinctively looked around before stepping out into the night.

At her place, she let him enter first. It was dead quiet inside, and it felt off to her. Was it just paralyzing fear? Or a gut feeling?

"I'll do a check," Jake said before she had a chance to suggest it again. He started upstairs, and she followed him. "Don't forget to check the closets," she said.

He opened the closet door in her bedroom.

"Be careful!" She hovered near the entrance to the bedroom.

He thoroughly searched the closet, along with every corner and room in the house.

Liz stayed close to him throughout, until he went down to the basement. She couldn't force herself to go down those stairs again. She preferred to wait at the top while he checked around down there.

Listening at the top of the stairs, she heard Jake moving around. Then a noise and a muffled moan from below. "Jake? What's going on down there? Are you okay?"

"Yeah," he sounded disgusted. "I stubbed my toe."

She waited for him. "Any heaters or paint cans down there?" she asked, trying to make light of her question by laughing half-heartedly, but she actually did worry that this house could get blown sky-high, too.

"No. Why do you ask that?"

"That's what was used to blow up my house in Bangor. You never know when he might use the same method again."

He'd climbed the stairs again and gave her a piteous look now, but was it concern for her safety or concern for her mental health? Her arms flopped limply at her sides.

She wanted him to know that she wasn't crazy, but how could she prove it? Sure, helping her out had been extremely kind, but she could tell that he didn't really believe her. He probably hadn't decided if she was lying or stark, raving mad.

Yet, he was still here.

The thing that really puzzled her—why did he want to help?

"The house is okay. I've also checked the locks on the doors and windows," he said, putting his hands on her shoulders and looking deeply into her eyes.

It screwed with her thought processes when he touched her. Just the touch, the heat of his fingers distracted her. To offset her mixed emotions, she casually picked a cobweb from his hair and took it to the garbage to escape the situation. If only he trusted her, believed in her.

"You okay?" he asked, dropping onto a wooden chair at the small table set in the kitchen.

"Why are you doing this?" she asked, keeping her back to him while she stared through the kitchen window into the dark. "You don't believe me, but you're willing to stay here tonight, sleep on my couch to allow me a good night's sleep?"

She liked him, but she couldn't trust anyone. What the heck? Now she didn't trust him, either? She rubbed her eyes. She had to let someone in, or she'd go insane. She turned to stare at him.

He cast a wry smile at her. The nicks on his poorly shaven chin gave him a bad-boy kind of look that went along with his current expression.

"You're tired, Liz. Have you looked in the mirror lately?" He leaned his elbows on the table and tipped his head. "You've got dark shadows under your eyes that have progressively worsened since you've been living here. You're losing weight," he said. "I just want to help out. Believe me, I have no agenda."

"Your way of being a good Samaritan?" she asked. "I don't mean to sound ungrateful, but I've had an issue with trust lately. If you're still willing to stay the night and let me sleep, I'm willing to accept that. I'm truly sorry you can't believe what I've told you without proof—but I don't blame you. This whole thing has been orchestrated so well, I barely believe it myself. On the other hand, I've never been distrusted by people before this weird stuff started happening. It's a new experience to me."

His stricken expression grew.

"This isn't a guilt trip. I don't blame you."

"At least we understand each other," he said. "If you just get me a blanket, I'll be all set and you can go get some sleep."

She found then handed over bedding and a pillow. Being caught testing the couch for comfort made him look guilty. "Don't worry, the lumps are in the right places."

She didn't laugh. She felt bad about causing him another restless night. And, upon closer examination, he looked a little tense.

"Liz, I'm sorry if I've hurt your feelings. I didn't do it purposely. I think you're a very special person. And I'm really glad that we met each other."

"You mean you do believe me?"

He looked serious. "It's just that I've seen no proof of anyone trying to hurt you. The things you've told me are hard to believe. Even you admit that."

"Did you look up the news reports about my house blowing up?" She pointed at his laptop.

He shook his head.

"Well! If you check, that'll prove my story."

He chewed on his upper lip for a few seconds, turned on his laptop and started searching. He found an article and began to read. "Liz, you didn't tell me they found the body of a woman in the house."

She felt her knees let go, and she dropped into the overstuffed chair next to the sofa. Her stomach lurched. "What? That can't be."

"I'm sorry, but this says the woman who owned that house died in the explosion."

"No, she didn't! I'm right here. This can't be happening," she said in a mere whisper. "Who died?"

"That's a good question," he said, but he was monitoring her closely. Reading her for believability, no doubt.

She bit her lip. "This just gets more and more complex. I might start wondering who I am myself if this person keeps making me look crazy."

"What about friends, relatives? They could vouch for you."

"We…" She paused. "That is, my parents and I lived in Europe until a couple of years ago. I finished my degree just before we moved to Bangor. I did get a job recently, but I didn't know my co-workers all that well."

He shook his head. "Damn. That won't help much."

Her parents had been fairly reclusive since her dad's retirement. There was always Maggie, their next-door neighbor. "We could call Maggie," she said and told him who the woman was.

He pulled out his cell phone. "Do you know her number?"

She recited the number by heart. He dialed. She waited impatiently. Finally, he ended the call and shook his head. "The number has been disconnected."

"She moved?" Liz tried to think. Maggie wouldn't just move away. "I don't understand."

He called directory assistance with no luck.

Where was Maggie? Good grief, not knowing many of her neighbors had seriously affected her now. Maggie had been the only person she and her parents had become friends with.

Next, her thoughts switched to the body found in the burned-out remains of her house. Had that person been inside her house when she'd walked through and into the backyard to check on the bird's nest? How had her attacker known she'd escaped if a body had been found in the ashes?

"I need more," Jake said. "Can't you give me something? Some proof that you're telling me the truth?

I haven't seen anything to believe you're being stalked."

"You haven't seen any proof of me hurting myself, either," she ground out, tapping her fingers on her leg. "But you're leaning in that direction, aren't you?"

He held his hands up. "I'm honestly trying to give you the benefit of the doubt. I want to believe you. You must know that. I'm here, aren't I?"

She stood, catching her pale, dark-eyed image in the mirror on the wall. She almost didn't recognize herself. She had to admit she was more tired than she'd ever been in her life. No sense trying to convince Jake tonight, because she was beyond thinking. She was too tired. "I'm going to bed now."

He crossed the room to her, but she didn't meet his gaze, because in her heart she knew he didn't believe her. And even though she couldn't blame him, she really wished he could.

"I'm going to be here all night. I won't leave. I promise I'll keep you safe," he said. His caring tone proved his sincerity.

"Right. Thanks." She needed some real sleep. But what about tomorrow and every night after that? She sighed and started toward the stairs.

"Maybe things will look brighter in the morning."

"Sure. And maybe this is all just a bad dream, and when I wake up again, I'll be at home in my bed. My parents will be alive and talking in the kitchen when I come downstairs. Mom'll have bacon and eggs cooking, and Dad will be whistling in the den," she snapped and regretted it instantly. She shook her head wearily. "You're right. I'm dog tired. I'd better go to bed."

In the darkness of her bedroom, the atmosphere in the house felt different tonight with Jake guarding her, even though he didn't believe her. She fluffed up her pillow, turned over and went to sleep.

The house was old and not very well insulated. Before she fell asleep, she heard him tapping away on his laptop.

The next morning she heard Jake moving around downstairs and she got up quickly. The aroma of bacon reached her as she padded across the room toward the bathroom. Her eyes watered. Had he cooked bacon because of what she'd said about her parents? Was he trying to make her feel better? She stopped and closed her eyes to hold back tears.

When she got downstairs, he said, "Hungry?"

"Mmmm, smells good." She crossed the kitchen and got a coffee cup from the cheap set of dishes she'd bought yesterday.

"Sleep well?" He flipped an egg like a pro then looked at her.

"Never better." He looked very comfortable in her kitchen. Dressed in shorts, a T-shirt and wearing her purple apron, he looked like he should be Mister June in a calendar of hunks. "Cute look for you." She grinned.

"I didn't want to get grease on my T-shirt." He looked embarrassed.

"Good idea."

They ate without talking much. She had to admit she felt a lot better today, especially since she'd slept well last night. She didn't think she'd even moved, she'd been so tired.

Jake looked at his watch, wiped his mouth with his napkin and stood. "I'd better get home and shower. I've got to pick up my files before I go to work." He stopped and eyed her. "Will you be okay?"

"I think I will," she said, following him to the door. "Thanks so much for letting me get a good night's sleep." She hesitated. "Things actually seem more controllable today."

"Don't worry, Liz. We're going to get this thing worked out."

She stepped outside and waited for him to go. Why did she feel that he believed her a little more today? "Did you find anything helpful on your computer last night?"

His eyes shifted away. "Not much, but I'll keep hunting."

She sighed. "I guess I'm not surprised. The police in Bangor couldn't find anything either, so don't worry about it. I appreciate the fact that you cared enough to look."

"See you later," he said, his shoulders taut when he crossed their yards.

On her run to the store for the paper, she saw it: her face on the cover of the Bangor Daily News, one of the many papers the store carried. Obviously, it was the biggest Bangor news of the day. Her gaze zipped over the article, which basically said that her remains were not the ones found in her burned house. Police were asking if anyone had seen her, stating that it appeared she'd used her passport to cross into Canada. There was no mention of the identity of the body found inside.

Maybe the time had come to call the police in Bangor again. She wasn't any safer in Canada than she had been in Maine. And even though Jake had helped her, she couldn't put his life on line by accepting his help.

It wasn't fair to him.

When she got home, she checked the house then went to the phone and called information for the number. The operator connected her to the police in Bangor.

"Bangor Police Department, state the reason for your call."

"Hello, this is Liz Davis calling. May I speak to Chief Hanlon?"

"One moment, please."

She was put on hold. She wiped at the perspiration beading on her forehead. She paced back and forth. She had a pain in her stomach, so she sat on the floor and pulled her legs up to her chest, then rested her head on her knees.

Was she in deeper trouble now? Would her stalker speed up his attempts to kill her once the Maine police knew she was still alive? Somehow, she had the feeling her troubles had just quadrupled.

"Hanlon here." His authoritative voice rankled.

"This is Liz Davis speaking, Chief." She waited expectantly, thinking he was going to be upset with her for not reporting everything to the police and leaving the scene of the crime.

"I'm so glad you called." He must have put his hand over the phone, but she could still hear his muffled voice as he hollered to a colleague that it was her on the phone.

"I saw the newspaper today. That's why I'm calling you."

"Where are you, Ms. Davis?"

"I'm in New Brunswick." No sense lying. They could track her call.

"Have you done something that you shouldn't have?" His voice was calm and steely.

"Apparently, breathing is my worst fault," she responded bitterly. "In case you haven't noticed, someone is trying to kill me. Don't forget my brakes were cut, then I was attacked inside my home. Then someone blew up my house. The only reason they failed is because I walked straight through the house and into the backyard to check on some baby birds." She gritted her teeth. "If I hadn't done that, you would definitely have found my remains in that building."

"Why didn't you come to us straightaway after the house was blown up?"

"Well, excuse me, but neither you nor Officer Spencer believed me when I said the second incident was more than a coincidence. I was scared, and I didn't know who I could trust. So I thought if I disappeared, I could try to find out why someone is trying to kill me."

"And did you?"

She sighed. "No. Nothing. But he's found me here in New Brunswick." Her voice wobbled as she tried to retain her composure. "I have nowhere to turn. I don't think I can protect myself from this person. He's very devious."

"You're saying 'he.' Do you know that for sure?"

"Well, it was a man who attacked me in my kitchen that night. And the lady next door saw a man skulking around my place the other day. Since I've been renting this house in New Brunswick, he seems to be able to get into my house whenever he wants to."

"I checked your background, Liz, at the time of the incidents and more thoroughly since your house burned. If someone wants to kill you, I can't, for the life of me, figure it out. If it's just a local nut, they don't usually go to the trouble of tracking their victim to another country. I'm not saying that isn't possible, mind you. Just not probable." He let out a long breath.

Liz choked out a laugh. "Can you try to figure it out, for the life of me?" she practically begged. Suddenly, something clicked with her. "Wait! You mean you don't believe that I left oily rags and a propane heater in the house? You knew someone tried to kill me then?"

"Of course. What happened at your house was just a little too convenient. One incident could be explained away maybe, but two coincidental occurrences and then your house blowing up? No, we are smarter than you think. We've been trying to find whoever is doing this to you. We might even have a lead. We didn't want the media to be aware of our ongoing investigation, so we let them run with the accidental-fire story. There's something else, we also found evidence that your parents' accident was caused because they'd swerved to avoid an animal. A witness just came forward. They weren't murdered."

"Thank you for that. You have no idea what that means to me," she breathed. Otherwise, she'd have been responsible for their deaths in a roundabout way.

At least the police believed her. Grief for her parents and thankfulness filled her. She so badly wanted to ask about the person found in the house but realized he wouldn't tell her anything about the ongoing investigation, especially if they didn't know who it was. And maybe she was afraid to find out who it was.

"So what do I do now?" Her spirits had definitely lifted. The police believed her!

"You're in grave danger. We wanted to keep the news about you being alive a secret, but you know how news people are, very dogged in their determination to find the truth. Is there anyone who can help you? You should come back here as soon as possible. Since you're out of our jurisdiction, we could call the police there and have them cooperate."

"No." She squeezed the phone tight. "I can't trust anyone I don't know, even the police. How do I know he couldn't impersonate them? He's practically invisible. I'll find my way back myself."

"We can make sure you see the photo of the officer you are to meet."

She took a deep breath and shook her head, even though he couldn't see her. "I've been able to keep myself alive so far. I just can't put myself in the hands of a stranger, even if he is a police officer. Whoever is after me has convinced me he's capable of just about anything. I hope I can make it back before the madman finds me again." Her voice wobbled. "At any rate, I'm on my way." She hesitated. "And Officer Hanlon?"

"Yes, my dear?"

"You don't know how much it means to me that you believe me. It gives me hope that we can catch this vile person."

"We'll catch him. You just be careful. And get yourself back here right away. Come straight to the station."

She hung up the phone and raced up the stairs to throw the few clothes she owned into a garbage bag. She took them to the car, re-entered the house and packed up the rest of the things she owned into a sad-looking little box. Even now fear was her shadow. But her will to survive proved stronger than fear.

She left a note for the landlord with the full month's rent and a promise to reimburse him for the rest of his expenses.

She thought about calling Jake before she left. The day had passed quickly. She hadn't realized it was nearly noon. She peeked out of the window and was surprised to see Jake's car in the driveway. He'd gone to work quite early, though. Maybe he'd taken the afternoon off?

A little voice inside her head told her to just go. Don't dawdle. You're on your own. You can call him and thank him when and if you ever get to Bangor.

Chapter Eight

Why couldn't he just believe her? He wanted to. He generally knew when people lied to him, and unless his radar had gone completely off course, she hadn't lied. She'd been telling him the truth—or what she believed to be the truth.

At the sound of a car door shutting outside, Jake crossed to the window and peered out. He'd decided to take a couple of weeks off at work.

Her car door hung wide open, but she wasn't around. Seconds later, she ran out of the house and she threw a box unceremoniously into the back seat of her car, jumped in and started up the engine.

Jake rammed his bare feet into sandals, ripped open the kitchen door and dashed across their yards. "Liz? What's going on? Where you going?"

Huge eyes met his, and her expression looked slightly panicked. She rolled down her window. "I've got to leave here right now!" She looked up and down the street behind her. "I wanted to thank you for everything you've done for me, but it's not a good time. You see, the Bangor police think I should leave here as soon as possible."

"Wait. You can't just leave." Liz needed his help, and he wanted to be the one to set her mind at rest.

"Don't you understand? It's not safe here," she said.

"But you were going to leave without saying good-bye?" Damn, he hated that this reality felt like a kick in the gut. "That's it? You're taking off without even telling me? You weren't even going to come to see me? Not even for a second?"

He could see her trying to decide what to do before she made her decision to stay even for a minute. He held her door open.

"Jake, I know you're not sure you can believe me, but my life is in danger. I honestly didn't want to go without thanking you properly, but every moment I stay puts me in more and more danger. And maybe it puts you in danger, too."

"I saw the newspaper today. I went to the international newsstand and got a copy of the Bangor News Daily." He trained his voice to come across as unaffected. "I took a couple of weeks off work. I hoped to help you solve your problem."

Her eyebrows went up. "It's because of that article that I'm in more danger than ever before. Since the police know I'm alive, my stalker might want to kill me in a hurry. Although I have no idea why."

"Just come inside for a minute. We should talk about this before you go off alone."

A tormented expression crossed her face, but she got out of the car and followed him to his place.

The minute she stepped inside, he closed the door and pulled her into his arms. His lips met hers in a demanding crush. He could feel her heart beating rapidly as he pulled her closer and ran his hands protectively across her back. He just knew he didn't want to lose her yet, and his feelings for her were undeniable.

She kissed him back until she finally shoved her hands against his arms and pushed out of his embrace. "No, Jake. I'm sorry, but I've got to go. My time is running out. Don't you understand? I'm running for my life." Her voice held a fevered pitch.

"And you're not going to do it alone," he said.

At first he thought he'd heard thunder rumbling outside. But when the whole house shook, he realized it had been an explosion in the driveway. That fact was verified by a piece of flaming metal smashing through his kitchen window and spinning wildly on his floor.

Liz screamed and dove into the corner.

Jake made a mad grab to get a pot of water to douse the hot steel before it ruined his flooring, or worse, set his house on fire.

Next, Jake looked through the smashed kitchen window at Liz's car, or what was left of it, Jake couldn't believe the remnants of her vehicle had quickly been engulfed in flames.

Guilt flooded him instantly. She'd legitimately needed help, and he'd suspected her of being either nuts or sick. He groaned. How stupid could he have been?

He pulled her out of the corner and wrapped his arms around her again. If he hadn't called her into his house, she'd be dead. She'd left the car running when she came inside. There must've been a timer set to go off while she drove away.

She knew it, too, because that reality lurked behind her eyes.

"Sit down right there, Liz." He led her to the kitchen chair farthest from the broken glass and still-smoldering steel. "I'm going to call 911, then get you some brandy."

After he made a quick call, she drank the tiny amount of brandy quickly, coughing a little afterward. She squeezed her eyes shut. She put her head down on the table and began sobbing quietly. "I'm not going to make it home. I can't do this by myself. That madman is going to get me."

Jake's muscles tightened in his back, and his hands clenched at his sides. He'd nearly lost another woman, a friend, through his own mistakes. He wouldn't do it again. At least he'd managed by the skin of his teeth to save her. Pure luck. From now on, he'd make sure luck had nothing to do with it. No one was going to hurt this woman, if his life depended on it!

Sirens roared in the distance, coming closer.

Liz sat up sharply. "I've got to get out of here. Now!"

"But the police are coming. I can help you explain," he said.

One perfectly shaped eyebrow rose. "Can you?"

He had the decency to look sheepish.

"Don't you understand?" She cleared her throat and paused for a moment before she spoke again. "This person will find me if I don't leave and quickly. Maybe the answer is in Bangor. Don't you see? Finally, the Bangor police believe me."

Damn it. She had a point. This guy was good enough to make it look like she'd been hurting herself. If she had died, no one would have believed her crazy stories about someone trying to kill her. "You're not going alone," he said.

"I've done it by myself up to now. I'll be okay." She made for the front door.

"Wait!" He grabbed her hand gently. "You don't have to do this alone any longer. I'm coming with you. Can you wait just a minute so that I can grab us a couple of jackets and get my wallet and passport?"

Her look of distrust made his gut wrench.

"It's too dangerous. I can't involve anyone else," she said, then realized. "Oh no! My wallet and passport were in the car."

"I don't blame you for not wanting me to help. But"—he hesitated—"I need to do this. And we can get you a temporary passport, but first we'll have to get to safety before we work out how we're going to do things."

She frowned at him, as if this time he'd lost his mind. "What are you talking about?"

"Just that I intend to do everything in my power to keep you safe. Why not let me? You don't have to do this alone, and you'll have a better chance if you have someone to watch your back."

She dragged in a ragged breath while she made up her mind about him. "You can come if you want to, but I'm doing this my way. Understand?"

He nodded. Man, she was one determined woman.

But could he blame her? He hadn't done much up to this point to prove that he was the guy she could count on. He had a chance to prove it to her now.

"Wait for me. I'll be right back." He ran up the stairs, quickly threw some clothes into a bag and jammed his wallet and passport into the back pocket of his jeans.

Liz was nowhere to be seen when he returned to the kitchen. For a moment, he thought she hadn't waited. His stomach lurched as he stared at the empty room.

"Liz?"

"I'm here," she whispered. He turned and saw her step out of the corner in the front hall.

Damn, he'd done the wrong thing again. He shouldn't have left her alone and afraid. He made a mental note not to let that happen again.

"I'm with you now." He held out his hand, and his heart clenched when she took it. He gently squeezed her vibrating hand. "We should go out the back door and stay low. Maybe we can slip out without being noticed."

"Good idea. We can go along the backyards for a while. Everyone will be out front looking at the car. That's how I got away in Bangor." She laughed, and he worried because there was a slightly hysterical note in it. "Who knows if it'll work twice?"

Liz yanked him along feverishly, and he thought about trying to slow her down, but she needed a sense of control right now.

"We can't go through backyards much longer. Someone is bound to see us," she said finally, slowing enough to look around.

"There's an alley over there," he said.

At this point, he figured she'd been going on pure adrenaline. She slowed down before they got to the entrance of the alley. He didn't like the pallor of her skin.

With a tight grip on her hand, he eased her to a stop. "I'm not going to let anyone hurt you again, Liz. You can¬ trust me."

Little curly tendrils of hair framed her face, damp from exertion. She offered a quick, forced smile while she monitored their surroundings.

He followed her gaze to the alley that led out onto the main street. Large elm trees created a canopy overhead, and trailing vines climbed the wooden fence on one side. A two-story brick building stood on the other side.

Obviously, she wasn't totally sure she could believe him. Maybe she thought he was just trying to placate her. Could he blame her? "Listen, we've got to find a place to hide. Then after dark, I'm going back to get my car," he said.

"No way. He'll follow you back!" Her voice rose with determination and fear.

"Don't worry. I'll make sure I'm not followed."

"You don't know how good this guy is. If you leave me to get the car, you'll never find me again. I'll be gone by the time you get back. I'm not going to sit and wait for you to bring that nut straight to me!"

"Okay, I'll think of something else then."

"I'm sorry. I know you're trying to help, but I'm not ready to turn my safety over to you or anyone else. After the explosion, I'm not even sure I want to turn myself over to the cops in Bangor. Maybe I should just try to disappear again."

"All the more reason to get transportation." He hoped she would get some color back in those chalky white cheeks. "We can't take public transportation if you don't know what this guy looks like."

* * * * *

She hated to admit he was right, but he made sense—they did need a vehicle. She couldn't agree with him about going back for his car, though. That would be tempting fate, and besides, she had a better idea. "Why don't we get Ada's car?"

He perked up at her suggestion. "Yeah, that's a good idea. Ada will lend us her car, and she can use mine in the interim."

"Let's hurry, then," she said, holding a hand out to him. "C'mon, he might not be far behind us."

Ada's house was a little story and a half not far from Jake's place. It looked exactly as Liz would have expected. A tiny garage sat next to a house decorated nicely with forest green wooden shutters. Flowers bloomed all around the front door, and a chubby, tattered-looking orange tabby cat cleaned himself on her front step as they slipped into her driveway, then crept around the house to her back door.

Even from outside, they could hear Ada singing country music at the top of her lungs. Jake knocked on her backyard patio door twice, but she didn't hear him. He looked at Liz, shrugged and opened the unlocked door.

"Jake! We're going to scare the poor woman witless!"

"Nah, she'll survive," he said confidently, but Liz noticed that he called out to her immediately, trying to get her attention before Ada saw them standing, unannounced, in her kitchen.

"Who's there?" Ada had been upstairs. She pounded down them quickly.

"It's Jake and Liz."

Dressed in her housecoat and slippers, her hair half-done up in curlers, she stepped onto the landing of her stairs overlooking the living room. She stood with a comb in one hand and a curler in the other.

"Jake? Liz? What's going on?"

"Ada, may I borrow your car for a few days?" Jake asked outright.

Liz sighed. He could have made a little small talk first rather than jump right in and scare her.

"Well, honey, you sure can." Ada pushed uncomfortably at her damp hair that wasn't yet totally in curlers. "Is there something wrong with your car?"

"No, it's fine. You can use my car. It's in the driveway at home."

"Your car is working?" she asked with a slight frown. "Then why do you want my car?"

Liz leaned closer to Jake. "Smooth. You're really good at this cloak-and-dagger stuff." For the first time in ages, she giggled, and it felt good to be able to make a joke in such dire circumstances.

Jake gave her a fake smoldering look.

"It's a long story. To tell you the truth, we can't really explain it right now. But I'd appreciate it if you'd lend me your car, no questions asked," he said.

Without hesitation, Ada stepped down the last two steps from the landing and went to her purse. She pulled out her car keys and handed them to Jake. "No problem."

He hugged her and kissed her cheek. "You're the best." He handed Ada his car keys and told her the car was still in his driveway.

She looked surprised by that but didn't say anything.

"One more thing, Ada. Will you call my office in the morning and tell them I'm taking an extra two weeks leave?"

"That's ripped it," Liz said under her breath when Ada's face instantly lit up.

"Oh my gosh, you two are eloping, aren't you?" Ada jumped up and down. Her rotund little figure practically jiggled while she expressed her glee. "I knew you two were right for each other from the start. Didn't I tell you that, Jake? Do you have time for tea and cakes before you go?"

"No," Jake began, then cleared his throat nervously. "We're kind of in a hurry."

A big grin crossed Ada's face. "I understand that. I was young once, too, you know." She hugged Liz and kissed her cheek. "Welcome to the family, sweetie. I'll be right back. I've just got to run upstairs and turn off the tap. I think I left the water running." She didn't give either of them an opening to explain what had really happened.

"We can't do this," he said out of the blue.

"I know what you're thinking," she said. "The attacker might hurt Ada." She grabbed his arm. "And, she's the only one who's ever seen him!"

"I'd never forgive myself if anything happened to her."

"Can't we take her someplace safe?" she said.

He nodded. "We'll have to tell her the truth."

When Ada returned, they told her everything. Her eyes widened as the sordid tale emerged. She just shook her head and tsked every time she looked at Liz. "You poor thing. Who would ever want to hurt you?"

"I don't mean to scare you, Ada, but we're worried for your safety, too. Where is Cameron?" Ada's husband often worked out of the country.

Ada picked at her apron. "He's visiting his brother in Denmark. He won't be back for two weeks."

"Okay, pack a quick bag. Is there anyone nearby who you can stay with?"

Ada nodded. "My sister lives outside the city. Don't just sit there, kids. Let's get a move on. I don't want anything to happen to you two. And Liz, I thought that man skulking around your place looked strange the other day, but I didn't want to scare you." She jumped up. "I'll go get my things." She left quickly and returned within minutes with a bag brimming full of clothing, her hair tucked neatly into the rest of the curlers. She was fast.

They got outside and before Ada climbed into the car, Liz said, "What about the cat?"

"Cat?" Ada said. "You mean the orange tabby that sits on my front porch?"

"Yes."

"He belongs to my next door neighbors. He likes to sun out there."

He put Ada's bag in the trunk of the car. Next thing Liz knew he'd disappeared. "Where'd Jake go?" she said to Ada.

When he rose next to the driver's side she realized that he'd been on the ground.

"What were you doing down there?" Liz asked, then instantly regretted the question because she realized why. Checking for a bomb. No sense to scare Ada any more than they needed to. "Oh never mind, I imagine you were just checking the tires?"

"A safety check is a good thing to do before hitting the road," he said, catching on to her meaning.

"Yeah, that's what I thought," said Liz.

Luckily Ada chatted away, unconcerned.

They dropped her off an hour later and got her safely inside. She waved at them from the door. Jake double-checked that they hadn't been followed before they drove away.

As if sensing her gaze on him, he turned and smiled at Liz. "We'll get through this."

Even though she returned the smile, she felt a sinking sensation. She hoped that he was right, but it all sounded too easy.

Chapter Nine

They pulled into a gas-stop restaurant and grocery store at three thirty in the afternoon. Liz's stomach had been grumbling for the last half hour, but she didn't complain.

He led her to a far corner in the restaurant where they could see everyone who entered and left.

"Let's have a big meal, so we don't have to stop again for a while," he suggested, opening his menu.

"Sounds like a good idea. Anyway, I'm starving."

Jake kept a keen eye on the door and the parking lot through the windows while they ate.

Taking the last sip of her tea, she stared at her lap and whispered, "I feel terrible that my purse blew up with my car this morning and I don't have any money. I promise to repay you for this when I can," she said, pushing at her hair and dreading the thought of what it probably looked like. And, much to her dismay, she spotted a big red stain on her jeans. "Great! I've got ketchup on my jeans," she moaned.

He picked up his napkin and wiped the edges of his mouth, effectively hiding the grin that lit his eyes. "You can rinse it off in the washroom before we leave."

She didn't want to make a big deal over a stain, especially considering everything they'd been through, but she must look like she'd just crawled out of a dumpster.

He reached into his pocket and pulled out his wallet to pay for their meal.

"I'll go to the ladies' room while you pay," she said. "Where do you want me to meet you?"

He looked suddenly conflicted about letting her out of his sight. "I'll wait outside the washroom door for you."

"I think I'll be okay to go to the washroom by myself. It is inside the restaurant, after all."

He stood and adjusted his shoulders, as if they were too tight for his own comfort. "Okay, meet me over on the grocery store side. I'll gas up then we can pick up some munchies so we won't have to stop again until we get to Bangor. Stay inside. You should be fairly safe with other people around you."

Liz went into the washroom and cringed at the sight in the mirror. She looked every bit as bad as she'd feared. She finger-brushed her hair and managed to get rid of most of the ketchup stain on her jeans.

Returning to the restaurant she immediately scanned the store for Jake. As he'd said, he'd waited there for her to make sure she was okay. "Now that you're here, I'm going to fill up the gas tank. Wait inside, okay?"

She nodded. "I'll browse while you do that. If I can borrow a little money, I need to buy a hairbrush and maybe a toothbrush."

"Of course. Just be cautious," he said, handing her a few bills and looking a little worried about leaving her inside alone.

She tucked the money into her back pocket and wandered toward the incidentals aisle where she'd most likely find the things she needed.

"Liz? Is that you?"

She turned quickly toward the familiar voice.

"Heaven save us, it is you!" He grabbed her and hugged her. "Why didn't you let us know that you were alive? Do you know how hard this has all been on Maggie?"

"Hugh?" Her next-door neighbor from Maine. His wife, Maggie, had saved her that night when the power had gone out. "What are you doing in New Brunswick?"

"We're on vacation, actually. Maggie was so distraught when you were thought to be dead, I couldn't console her. I finally convinced her to come here on a mini-vacation. She's never seen the bridge to Prince Edward Island, so we decided to check it out."

His clothes definitely indicated he was on vacation. She'd never seen him dress like this before. He had on a loose, flowered shirt and a pair of khaki shorts. She cringed inwardly at the sight of his black socks and leather sandals. Cute! she thought. The look suits you, Hugh.

His nearly bald pate shimmered bright red under the fluorescent lighting of the store. Looked like he had quite a sunburn.

He pulled on her arm. "C'mon, honey. Maggie will just flip to see you. It'll make her vacation a hell of a lot more enjoyable if she sees you alive and kicking."

Liz balked. Standing her ground, she glanced outside at Ada's vehicle sitting at the pumps. Jake wasn't there. Maybe he was double-checking under the car again.

"No, I can't. I'm waiting for a friend. He should be here any minute."

"Aw, c'mon." He pointed. "See? The car's just right there."

She looked out into the parking lot. She didn't see his car. "Where?" she asked, pressing her face against the window. "I don't see it."

He stretched around the corner of the shelving. "Oh, I guess you can't see it from here. We parked at the side of the building so I could check one of the tires. Come on, Maggie will be so happy to see you," he implored.

With one last look around, and no one strange watching her, she decided to take a chance. After all, she knew Hugh and even though she didn't like him much, she adored Maggie. She hated the thought of

Maggie suffering over her supposed death. She should have contacted the dear woman, but her phone had been out of order or disconnected. And this was Hugh, Maggie's husband, after all. "All right, but I can't be long. My friend will wonder where I went."

She followed Hugh out the door. Funny, Jake was nowhere to be seen. Something didn't feel right. Why would he leave her alone for so long? At least if she stayed with Hugh, she wouldn't be alone until Jake found her.

"The car is here, just around the corner," he said, taking her hand and pulling her with him. "Maggie! Look who's here," he called out.

Liz frowned and looked at the black van with a rental sticker in front of her. She didn't see anyone in the vehicle, but the back windows had a very dark privacy tint on them. Maybe she just couldn't see through them.

Hugh slid open the back door, and Liz leaned forward to look inside. Before she could turn and ask Hugh what was going on, a strange-smelling cloth clamped over her mouth and nose. She tried to fight and scream, but the cloth muffled her voice, then everything started to go black until…nothing.

* * * * *

Jake groaned and touched the back of his head. It felt like it had been cracked wide open. He'd woken to find himself sprawled across the concrete next to his vehicle, a stranger leaning over him.

"You okay, bud? What happened to you?"

"You didn't see the guy hit me?" He swiped grit off his cheek.

The stranger shook his head but instantly looked alarmed. "Want me to call the cops?"

Jake touched the spot on his head where he'd been hit. His hand came back covered with blood.

He felt a little disoriented at first, his vision blurring off and on. When he could finally manage to sit up, his head pounded as if someone was still hitting him. A feeling of nausea welled up in his stomach, and he took several deep breaths to quell the sick feeling. "No. I don't have time," he said.

Then it all came back to him. "Liz!" He tried to stand but fell back to his knees. He closed his eyes and used every bit of strength he could muster to stand. His vision blurred again, and for a moment the world spun. He leaned over and grabbed the car door. After a couple of minutes, things began to clear. Except for his mammoth headache.

Who had hit him? Stupid question. He knew who it had to have been. But where had he come from? Jake hadn't even seen his attacker. Liz had warned him about that, hadn't she?

He glanced down at his watch. How long had he lain there? Surely not long.

With an ever-sinking feeling, he made for the grocery store. Unfortunately, he found exactly what he'd expected to find inside. Nothing. Liz had disappeared.

He held on to his bashed head and tried to focus. He'd fucked up royally, and Liz was in the hands of the madman trying to kill her. Jesus, Mary and Joseph, he'd promised to keep her safe. He asked everyone inside and out, but no one had noticed her leaving.

Shit! Shit! Shit! His hands clenched at his sides, and his teeth fused together. "If you hurt one hair on her head, you're going to pay, you bastard," he mumbled under his breath on his way back to his vehicle.

Nearing panic, he noticed a young man hitchhiking on the main road near the gas station.

He ran to the side of the road. "Excuse me, I'm looking for my friend. Did you see a woman with long blond hair leaving the gas station? Maybe with another man?"

The hitchhiker looked older close-up. His eyes were bloodshot, and his lips were cracked. He nodded and held out a filthy hand. "First, have you got any money?" the man said.

"Did you see her or not?"

The guy nodded but kept his lips tight and his hand out.

Jake's gut turned to rising lava, but he grabbed his wallet and handed the guy a ten. The man continued to hold out his hand. Jake slapped another ten on top of the first one.

"I saw her," he said, cramming the money into his jacket. "Yeah. I thought it was kind of funny when she fainted outside the van. The man picked her up and shoved her inside. He had a cloth or something in his hand when he turned around. He gave me a weird look when he saw me watching him." The hitchhiker yanked at his jacket as if it were suddenly too tight. "Gave me a funny feeling, like I'd just witnessed something that I shouldn't have, but I wasn't sure." He suddenly looked worried that he'd witnessed a crime and failed to report it.

Jake put his hand to his forehead and looked down at the ground. A million terrifying scenarios ran through his skull.

"Hey, you're bleeding."

"Did you get the license plate number?"

"No. It was a Prince Edward Island license, though. I did notice that. It was a black van. Ford, I think."

"How long ago?" He had no idea how long he'd been knocked out.

"Not long. Five minutes tops." The man pointed in the direction that the van had gone. "If you drive fast, you'll probably catch them."

Jake tore back to the car. Each time his feet pounded into the pavement, jagged knives of pain seared through his head.

If they had only a five-minute lead, he had a chance to catch them. They were headed north, deeper into Canada, not back toward the States.

He jumped into his car and spun out on the highway, covering the hitchhiker in choking dust. As he sped along, he prayed he didn't get pulled over by the police. Thankfully, on this twinned highway he was able to pass everything in sight for a while. But then the road narrowed and the older section of highway became one lane. His muscles tightened, and his lungs threatened to cut off his breath. Had the hitchhiker given him the right information? He hadn't spotted a black van yet.

He'd just started to think about going back when suddenly he spotted the van ahead of him. About four vehicles away. He squeezed the steering wheel and pressed his foot onto the gas pedal to keep up with the van. He passed two vehicles but left one between them in hopes he wouldn't be noticed. He'd stay here unless the driver slowed his speed and made Jake fall behind.

Chapter Ten

Liz fought a leaden lethargy to open her eyes. The taste of garlic lingered at the back of her mouth, and twin ice picks chiseled behind her eye sockets. She tried to stretch, to move, but found herself trussed tightly. Her mouth had been taped, too. She felt panicky for a second but managed to calm her breathing enough to get air through her nostrils.

From where she lay across the back seat she could see Hugh's red pate over the headrest of the driver's seat. Her eyes flashed to the passenger seat. No sign of Maggie. Surely, Maggie was at home and completely unaware of what was going on. But why had the phone been disconnected? She couldn't bear the thought of her friend being connected to this. Worse, it must have been Hugh in her kitchen that night. She should have recognized his body odor! But why?

"So, you're coming around, eh?" He sounded slightly inebriated. He picked up a flask and took a noisy swig to prove the point.

She wiggled to loosen her bindings and tried to talk, but her voice only made a muffled sound through the tape.

His crude laugh proved he enjoyed her discomfort. "You might as well calm down for a while longer. You'll just get yourself all flustered and upset. I don't think it'd be very comfortable to be trying to breathe with your mouth taped up if you start blubbering."

Liz thought about what he'd said. Unfortunately, it made sense. At the moment, there was nothing she could do but lay there and try to think of a way to escape.

What had happened to Jake? Why hadn't he shown up? She closed her eyes and tried not to panic when she realized that Hugh might have gotten to him first. Was she breathing too fast through her nose? Her lungs felt like they were going to burst.

Jake had to be okay. He had to.

She felt herself falling again into a deep, dark hole.

When she woke again, the van was driving over an extremely bumpy road.

Hugh leaned around the seat and looked back at her. The way he scanned her body scared her more than the thought of dying. This was Maggie's husband? The man who'd barely spoken to her?

"They wanted me to take you straight back to Bangor and kill you there." He returned his attention to the road as he hit an exceptionally big pothole. "But I'm not going to do that until I've had my fun. Been waiting for this for two months. And you're not going to be able to squawk about it—not where anyone can hear you, anyway." His laugh turned her blood to ice.

They rode along for at least another ten minutes before the van lurched to a stop. Liz tried to break the tape on her wrists, but she only managed to exhaust herself even more. The drug must've sapped her energy.

She waited while Hugh jumped out. The next thing she knew, his grubby hands pulled her roughly out of the back seat. She couldn't kick at him because her feet were taped. She could only wriggle like a fish out of water.

The smell of his foul liquored breath made her feel sick. He threw her over his shoulder and carried her to a decrepit-looking camp in a heavily forested area. She looked around to see any other camps nearby. Nothing.

Though squat and chubby, Hugh's strength didn't falter while he lugged her to the cabin. She'd have a hard time fighting him even if she got free, but that didn't deter her. In fact, she'd learned a little self-defense from her father. Something they'd always joked about because he taught her a few basic moves before she'd started dating. Not that she'd dated much. She racked her still-fuzzy head to try to remember what some of the best tactics were, other than the obvious one she couldn't wait to try—a good swift kick to his nether regions.

He'd been doing well until he dropped her onto the ground outside the cabin so he could open the door. She grunted as the air rushed from her lungs and her teeth jarred together. Her hip pained as it smashed into the exposed root of a tree. The smell of dank earth shoved into her face and permeated her nostrils. She squirmed and tried to kick him again.

"Oh, you're scaring me. Please don't kick me." He laughed wickedly and then rammed his shoulder into the door and broke the lock.

Next he grabbed her roughly and yanked her off the ground by her arms before dragging her backward into the building. Rocks and twigs dug into her along the way. Every bone in her body ached, but she tried to stay alert to her surroundings—just in case.

When he finally dragged her all the way up the rotted wooden steps, jarring her back and shoulders on every step, he dropped her hard onto the dirty cracked linoleum floor of the camp. Pain seared her backbone, and her eyes watered.

Making a disgusting sound of intent, he reached down and yanked the tape off of her mouth, bringing more tears to her eyes. "Why are you doing this?"

He sneered at her and laughed. "Are you really that dense? I'm doin' this because I get paid to. It's my job."

"What do you mean?"

He lumbered around the cabin, kicked a chair out of his way, then grinned down at an old worn couch. "I mean, I make big money getting rid of people. It's my chosen occupation."

Her blood ran cold. "You're a...a...hit man?"

He reached into his pocket and pulled out a gun with a silencer on it, shaking it in the air in front of her before he pointed it at her face.

She closed her eyes and silently asked for help. Nothing happened. She opened her eyes and looked at him again.

"Don't get your panties in a wad. I'm not killing you yet. I don't like havin' my fun with the girls after I kill 'em, now do I? I'm not that sick." He grabbed the waistband of his pants and pulled them up. "Bad enough, I'm going to lose my bonus because I couldn't make it look like an accident. You must have a horseshoe up your butt." He grinned, showing small, uneven teeth. "But then I'd have missed out on all of the fun, wouldn't I? That'll be a better bonus."

Liz tried to swallow, but her throat had gone completely dry. "What about Maggie?" She needed to distract him and thought the topic of his wife might work. Maggie was the first person who popped into her head.

"What about her?" Hugh sneered.

"Is she involved in all of this, too?"

He looked theatrically shocked. Bastard!

"Dear sweet Maggie? How could you even think such a thing? That fat cow'd sooner slit my throat than let me put one little finger on you."

Her plan wasn't working. It seemed to be getting him even more worked up. He took the pistol with the silencer and threw it on the counter top across the room and took a step toward her lying on the filthy floor.

"Does she know what you do?"

"Fuck no! She's been the bane of my existence. Having to pretend to love her and act the happy, married husband as a cover to my real occupation was beginning to wear very thin. I thought I'd had it made when my target lived next door, though. Should've been my easiest job."

Liz closed her eyes for a second. Poor Maggie. She flashed her eyes open again when she heard the floorboards creak under Hugh's dumpy weight.

She cringed back, but instead of jumping her bones, he took out his flask and drank deeply from it. He wiped his mouth with the back of his hand after he'd emptied it. His lascivious gaze ran the length of her, coming back to the place where her blouse had been partially ripped open while she was being dragged into the camp.

Change the subject, Liz, and quick! She racked her brain for something good.

"If you're a hit man, who hired you to kill me?"

Her question seemed to distract him. His expression changed, and he remained silent for a few minutes before he spoke. "What difference does that make?"

"If I'm going to die, at least tell me who wants me dead." She gave him a hostile glare that only seemed to give him more enjoyment. "And I'd like to know how you became a hit man. You don't seem the type," she lied.

"Well, what if I tell you that your father hired me? How would that make you feel?"

"My father's dead, as you well know," she spat out at him.

"Do I now? Your adoptive father is dead. But your real father is alive and kicking. And he doesn't want you around." Hugh dropped onto a rickety chair next to her and stretched his words out in a childish taunt.

"I don't believe you!"

"As if I care if you believe me or not." He licked his lips and reached down and ran a rough finger between her exposed breasts. "Soft skin. Never had a blonde before." His stubby fingers yanked another button open, exposing even more of her flesh.

She tried to wrench away from his filthy, groping hands, but couldn't. "Just kill me and get it over with!" Her mouth tasted like dirt and felt as dry as sand. She hated the fact that her panicking made her gasp for breath. That obviously excited Hugh more, because he watched her heaving chest with too much interest.

Finally, he tore his gaze away. "Stop teasing me! I'm not going to kill you—yet. Not until I've had my fun, at least. Mind you, I usually prefer my entertainment quite a bit younger than you." He leered down at her, pulling his leather belt off as he spoke. "But you'll do in a pinch."

Liz instantly screamed. She continued screaming over and over until she was hoarse, and tears streamed down her face.

He watched her with a sick grin on his face. "You just go ahead and tire yourself out." He now stood with one leg on each side of her trussed-up form. "The more you scream now, the less you'll be able to scream later."

"You miserable old pervert." The words came out ravaged and rough, and she hated that he was right. She'd tired herself considerably.

"Sticks and stones..." He laughed, then to Liz's surprise, he stepped over her and walked to the window and looked out.

Maybe there were other camps in their vicinity, after all? Was he worried that someone had heard her?

He left the building without even giving her a backward glance. Time ticked by miserably while she worked frantically to free herself. Too soon, the sound of the van door shutting and footsteps crunching back to the cabin made her body begin to shake.

Before she had a chance to squirm a foot, he'd returned to the cabin. The door hanging half off its hinges wobbled and squeaked, but Hugh managed to yank it shut.

Another pint of vodka hung from his grubby hand. Hopefully, that'd give her a little more time to make her escape.

"My hands and feet hurt. Can't you loosen the bindings just a little?" she asked.

He scowled at her, until a disgusting grin spread across his meaty face. "In a while, I'll be taking the binding right off your feet, so quit complaining." He crossed the room and sat at an old metal table where he could watch her while he drank straight from the bottle.

"How do you know my real father?" She tried to calm her voice and make it sound like she really was interested in his story. And that she actually believed him! More important, why would some guy who professed to be her father want her dead?

Hugh belched and rubbed his face with his hand. "Your pop's an important man. Why would he want a little pain in the ass like you around? If you turned up, it would be very inconvenient for a man like him. Could cause him all sorts of trouble."

"I have no intention of finding my birth father. My adoptive parents were everything to me. I don't care a whit about him—I can promise you that." She could feel her parents turning in their graves at her pretense. They were her parents—there was no one else.

"Don't care. I've been paid to do this job, and I've never disappointed a client yet. I'm not about to start now. You've given me enough trouble. Your death was supposed to look like an accident." He slammed the pint down on the table. "I don't appreciate being made to look like a failure."

His cold eyes strayed to her opened blouse again, inciting icicles to form in her blood. She had to keep him talking. Since they'd arrived at the cabin, he'd drained the second bottle of booze. "So this man, my…"—she faltered—"father is afraid I'll ruin what? His marriage? His career? I don't understand."

"You certainly don't understand." Hugh's voice slurred a little more. "If you don't disappear, there'll be a lot of money that my client won't receive. He can't take that chance. You're a liability, bitch."

Even if she had been adopted, which she wasn't, why would anyone want her dead? It didn't make sense. Did they have her mistaken for someone else?

Hugh shook his empty bottle. "After you meet this man, and I've dumped your body, I'll make so much money I'm going straight to Rio for gambling and fun in the sun," he said, his voice slurred.

"What about Maggie?"

He snorted so loud she thought he'd choked. If only!

"My dear, loving wife has served her purpose. And she was the biggest pain-in-the-ass busybody. Nearly blew my cover a couple of times. Might have made a small mistake in making her part of my cover." He gritted his teeth, then laughed low in his throat this time. "The ol' bat's in the ashes of your house now. She wanted to be over there so often, thought I'd let her stay there forever."

Liz's lungs froze, and the room darkened. The body found in her house had been Maggie. Maggie! "Oh God, no! How could you? She doted on you. She waited on you hand and foot."

"Stupid of her, wasn't it?" His reddened eyes glowered at her, and his head began to hang heavily.

Liz swallowed hard. She'd never be able to appeal to Hugh's sense of decency, because he had none. Not a shred. She couldn't imagine how Maggie had lived with this monster without seeing the devil inside.

Or maybe she had and that's why he killed her.

* * * * *

Jake had followed the van for ages, fairly certain he hadn't been seen. Still, he remained cautious and stayed far enough back that the driver wouldn't get suspicious.

Liz might already be dead, but he refused to accept that fact until he found her. Besides, her attacker could've killed her fairly quickly in the parking lot, but since the hitchhiker saw a cloth in his hand, Jake had to hope the bastard had only drugged her.

There'd been too many witnesses at the gas station for the abductor to take any chances.

In his rush to get Liz to safety, he'd left his cellphone at home. It had been stupid of Jake not to tell someone to call the police back there. But, if he'd wasted precious time, he'd never have caught up to them.

On the road ahead of him, the kidnapper's brake lights jittered then turned solid before taking a right down a dirt road into a heavily wooded area.

Jake gritted his teeth.

Right now he prayed he'd done the right thing. Odds of success weren't exactly in his corner. But maybe, as a man who was crazy about Liz and would do anything to save her, he had momentum and reason to be successful.

It didn't take long to realize it took nerves of steel to remain out of sight and risk losing them. He kept his windows down and listened to the vehicle creaking over the rutted road ahead. Suddenly, he inched the car around a corner. Thick alders grew up on both sides of the dirt road and scraped the fenders of the car for a mile before he left the rutted path and came to a fork that went off in three directions. The van had disappeared. Sweat broke out on Jake's forehead. Which way had they gone?

He got out of the car and listened for any sound of a vehicle traveling ahead. It seemed like the countryside had come alive with sounds. Birds twittering, wind rustling the leaves of the trees, all of it blocking his attempt to hear what he really wanted to hear—a car bumping over the rutted dirt road.

Even the sun seemed against him. The days were just starting to get longer, and the sun's lower position in the sky made it hard to see. He had to find her. If he took the wrong road he'd waste precious time.

Worse, the hard-packed ground had been baked dry, leaving no chance for fresh tire tracks.

A faraway sound twigged his hearing. At first it sounded like a bird in the forest beyond, but it quickly turned into screaming. Hair rose on the back of his neck, and his hands went instantly clammy.

He jumped into the car and gunned the engine until he practically sailed over the rutted tracks, the vehicle landing with a bone-jarring crunch after every launch. He prayed the sounds weren't echoing and luring him in the wrong direction. He had to slow down now since the road had gotten narrow. He was afraid he might burst around a corner and let them know he was there before he was ready.

Inching the vehicle around a particularly sharp curve, he finally spotted the black van next to an old, dilapidated camp. He slowly brought the car to a stop and backed it up and parked behind bushes, so it couldn't be seen.

Throwing the car door open, he slid out and raced through the woods, circling around to the back of the camp through dense underbrush. Alders and thorns whipped and scratched him, but he barely felt his skin being slashed. His mind was on one thing, saving Liz.

She hadn't screamed again, and that worried him.

He stopped and stood, unmoving, when the man who'd kidnapped Liz came out of the camp and got a bottle out of his van. Jake silently cursed himself for not being closer at that very moment. It would have been a good opportunity to tackle the bastard, but since he had no idea if the guy had a weapon, he'd have to be smart about his attack.

When the kidnapper went back inside, Jake got close enough to a window at the side of the building to hear Liz talking, trying to calm her abductor. She was alive! He blessed her for being intelligent enough to try to keep the bastard occupied and calm. Unfortunately, shabby curtains covered the window, so he couldn't see her.

He moved forward. Crows lifted off from a nearby tree, cawing in unison. He froze again. Had the damned birds just given him away? He listened intently. No one came. And inside, even though the bastard taunted Liz, she kept her cool.

Luckily the next window had no curtain. Peering quickly through the dust-covered pane over the kitchen sink, Jake managed a look. Liz was tied up and lying on the floor, while the bastard drank from a bottle at the kitchen table and stared at a piece of paper before crumpling it and shoving it back into his pocket.

Jake turned away and pressed his head against the weathered wooden shingles and exhaled slowly. He'd also seen a gun on the counter. No way he could get through the door before the man grabbed the gun and shot him. Or Liz.

His fists clenched, and he knew that he would feel great satisfaction when he rammed his closed hand into that ugly face.

Chapter Eleven

Liz waited and watched Hugh's eyelids flutter before his head lolled forward. When his eyes finally closed, and he began to snore, she tried to shuffle her way to the door. Unfortunately his eyes flashed open again, and he shook a spastic finger at her. "I wouldn't try that if I were you." His voice slurred drunkenly. "After I have a little bit of a rest, you and I are going to taaangggo." His sagged, but he managed to raise it and peer at her through half-closed eyelids again. "On the other hand, why wait? I'll just help myself now. And again later.

He staggered before jerking forward into a partial crouch to try to undo the tape on Liz's legs.

Her legs were free. Crap! Her plan to kick him senseless the moment the tape was free couldn't work because they were numb. She couldn't even lift her feet right now, let alone fight him.

Hugh fell onto his knees and heaved himself on top of her. Air whooshed out of her lungs, and her ribs felt like they'd been cracked in two.

He mauled at her arms with fumbling hands. Raising her still-taped hands above her head, he managed to hold them there with one hand while his putrid, panting breath washed over her.

She turned her head to try to escape his searching foul mouth.

"You dirty bastard," she said. "I hope you rot in hell!"

A guttural laugh erupted. "If this ain't heaven, I don't know what—" Unexpectedly, he grunted and flew off her sideways, landing in a heap near the old kitchen table.

A silhouette stood over the drunken sod. She squinted. "Help me," she said instantly, then realized it was Jake. Oh, thank God!

She loved every inch of that warrior expression. "Jake! How'd you find me?"

But Jake was busy. Too busy to talk, since he immediately dove after Hugh on the floor and smashed his fist hard into Hugh's crumpling face. It seemed that Jake quickly had the upper hand until Hugh rallied and landed a lucky punch that managed to stun Jake for a moment.

After that punch, Hugh staggered to his feet. Jake shook his head and blinked his eyes, all the while trying to get to his feet. Had he hit his head against the table when he fell?

Hugh made a disjointed dash for the cupboard.

"There's a gun over there," Liz screamed, rolling sideways. With her hands still trapped, she pushed herself off the floor. Icicles of pain attacked the nerve endings in her feet and she'd barely managed to stand.

Before Hugh got the gun, Jake yanked him backward, but he didn't look solid, and he had blood trickling down his neck from the back of his head. He'd been injured.

Meanwhile, Hugh elbowed him in the gut so hard that Jake doubled over and fell to the floor again. Hugh laughed and grabbed the gun from the cupboard.

"You just couldn't keep out of this, could you, lover boy?" He pointed the gun at Jake's head and turned his attention to Liz. "How much do you want him alive?" His eyes narrowed. "Unbutton your blouse."

Liz gawked at him. No, he couldn't do this to her.

He shook the gun in Jake's direction. "Go on. Do it now, or lover boy gets an extra hole in his head."

Liz's shaking fingers instantly went to the buttons on her blouse, and she tore her gaze away from Jake's pale face. Her wrists were still taped tightly, so it wasn't easy to work her fingers, but she had to try.

The sun was setting, and long shadows had crept into the cabin.

"Damn, I can't see good enough," Hugh said, still pointing the gun at Jake. He inched away and lit a lantern on the table with his lighter.

Jake definitely had blood trickling down the side of his face, and he appeared to be stunned.

"Get at it, little lady, or you'll get to see the color of the stuff inside your boyfriend."

"You want a show, Hugh?" she said, angry but aware of what she had to do. "Well, I'm going to give you a show. Gee, too bad you don't have any music. I'm much better when I do it to music."

Hugh's eyes popped momentarily. "Yeah, right, I wasn't born yesterday, you know."

"How do you think I put myself through school? My adoptive parents didn't have much money, now did they?"

Hugh would probably believe that about her father. Being in the military wasn't a ticket to the high life. In fact, she'd been lucky enough to get a small scholarship toward her university education. She'd heard her parents fighting one night. Her mother thought they should accept money from some unknown source and make things easier for Liz. But her father had been adamant. "She's got to learn to cope with life. It's the best gift we can give her," he'd said. Liz silently agreed and never told them she'd heard the argument. She knew her parents couldn't afford the tuition, and she hadn't been about to let them put themselves in debt by borrowing the money for her.

She held her taped hands out. "Undo me and I'll do a striptease that'll drive you wild."

"I'm not that stupid!" For a moment, Liz feared he wouldn't fall for it, until he turned to Jake and said,

"You take the tape off her." With the gun still aimed at Jake, he motioned for him to untie her. "And no funny stuff or your little stripper here is going to die before your eyes."

Jake stumbled over to her and leaned in to take the tape off. Liz couldn't believe her luck. "I'm going to distract him any way I can. Be ready to grab the gun," she whispered as quietly as she could.

He blinked his eyes and shook his head, trying to shake off his lethargy. "No."

"Hey! What are you saying?" Hugh staggered over and pushed the gun against her temple. "No funny stuff or somebody's going to die."

"I just didn't want him to get too upset and get himself shot," she said, flashing her eyes innocently at Hugh. "He only likes me to do this for him."

Hugh swallowed loudly, an excited gleam appearing in his eyes. Liz could see that he was falling for her story. Must be the booze fogging his brain.

She frowned at Jake, who still wasn't playing along. "You promise you won't get upset and get yourself shot, baby?" she said louder than usual, putting more emphasis on her words.

Jake glared at her. It was obvious he thought she was insane, but his reaction must have made Hugh think she was telling the truth, because he suddenly forgot to aim the gun.

"Hot damn. I didn't count on this." He knocked Jake to the floor again with the gun and pulled a chair over and sat down in front of her. "Get to it. We don't have all day."

Liz gyrated slowly, moving to tacky music she imagined in her mind. Meanwhile, Jake rubbed the back of his head and stayed down. From this angle she could see his head had been cut and he was still bleeding heavily. No wonder he'd been slow to action. She hoped he'd be able to grab the gun.

Her hands, though still numb, were able to fumble open a couple more buttons.

"You're not so great at this," Hugh said. He sounded like he was starting to lose faith in her promises.

"I can't help it," she said. "My hands are numb from being taped so tight. Maybe you'll have to unbutton my blouse for me," she said, swallowing hard. She gave him as sexy a smile as she could without throwing up. She almost physically retched, but managed to gain control again.

"I'll have to put the gun down for that," Hugh said, an untrusting leer crossing his features.

For a moment, Liz thought he wouldn't go for it, and she leaned ever so slightly forward to give him a better view of her cleavage. The temptation must have been too much for him. He pulled the kitchen table close and laid the gun down.

"C'mon, baby, let's see what ya got." His grubby fingers snagged her blouse and worked clumsily at the next button. He practically panted with excitement.

Liz shot Jake a get-ready look. He nodded slowly in agreement. She gyrated closer and closer to Hugh, bending over so that he could look down her blouse again. "It's no use. My hands are completely numb. You'll have to undo all my buttons."

Her skin crawled. Before he got her blouse completely open, she took a few steps back and tried to dance the way she'd seen an actress do in a movie. Competent or not, the motions kept Hugh's attention and gave Jake time to recover a little. Hugh's eyes narrowed on her, and his expression made her taste bile.

"Am I going too slow?" she asked, hating every second of her attempt to distract him. "Jake and I like to take it off faster than this, and he likes to help me undress," she began, reaching up and lowering one bra strap under her blouse, pulling her bra down just enough that he could see the swell of her breast before she pulled the strap back up again.

This time Hugh lunged at her, both hands pawing the air. She sidestepped and dove for the table, knocking the gun into the far corner of the room.

Slower than she expected, Jake finally got up to attack. Hugh still didn't realize what was going on. He still wanted her.

Jake jumped Hugh, but not in time to stop Hugh's filthy hands from touching her breast inside her bra.

That felt even dirtier than when she'd danced for the pervert. She didn't know if she'd ever feel clean again.

Jake seemed stronger now. The break had allowed him to come around. He pounded Hugh three times in the face. Hugh dropped like a hunk of beef. Either from the booze or the punches, he'd passed out. Jake raised his fist to pound him again.

"Stop, Jake. He's out. Let's tape him up. You don't want to kill him." She put her half-numb hands on both sides of Jake's fist, and she could feel the tension behind his muscles.

A low growl came out of Jake, a tortured sound. He grit his teeth. "But I do want to kill the dirty bastard."

"No, you don't." Liz handed him the duct tape that Hugh had used on her. "Tape him up, tight."

* * * * *

After Jake had Hugh trussed so tightly he'd never get out, he noticed the scrap of balled-up paper on the floor. It was the same one Hugh had been reading earlier. It must have fallen out of his pocket during the scuffle. He snatched it up and shoved it into his pocket. No time to look at it now. He had to get to Liz before she fell apart.

She'd moved to lean against the kitchen cupboard but ran her newly released hands up and down arms that crossed her chest protectively. She'd buttoned her blouse to the very top button, and when his gaze wandered to her, she gave him a strange look. Agonizing over what she'd done, she wondered if he understood her turmoil.

"Liz, don't do this to yourself," he said, managing to wrap her in his arms, even though she didn't welcome him at first. He kissed the top of her head. Finally, she grinned at that, knowing her hair had to be full of pine needles and dirt, but he'd still kissed her.

She shuddered and pressed her face into his broad shoulder. In response, his arms wrapped tighter around her.

"That was the most vile, disgusting thing I'll ever do in my life," she said between hitching breaths.

"I wanted to rip him apart with my bare hands. Thankfully, you stopped me. He'll get what's coming to him. In prison."

Hugh began to moan. "He's coming around," Liz said, tightening her grip on Jake's arm.

"We need to get him to the police," she said. "He told me he's a hit man." Her voice sounded tight and constricted even to her. "Someone hired him to kill me."

"Why? Who would hire him to kill you?"

"I have no idea. He said it was my birth father. But he's lying. My father died in a car accident."

"I want you to wait in Ada's car," Jake said, his words calm and calculating.

"Why?"

"I want to have a little chat with Hugh before we take him to the police."

"You're not going to kill him." Her eyes panned the room for the gun that she'd sent flying. It was still on the floor in the corner.

"No, but I'm going to find out who hired him, and he may wish he were dead before I'm done," he ground out.

"You can't do that."

Jake looked into her eyes. "Trust me. I'll stop before he dies." He winked at her, and she sucked in a quick breath. He'd said that for Hugh's benefit. He wanted to scare him into spilling his guts. He was playing her game, only this time the tactic was fear rather than seduction.

"Wait in the car, Liz," he added.

"Don't let him do this," Hugh blubbered. Jake had been right, Hugh had been listening all along.

Liz nodded and looked into Jake's endearing face. Dirt smudged over his cheekbone, and blood had started to dry in the rivulets that had dripped onto his face. What would have happened to her if she hadn't met him? If she'd moved into a house somewhere else?

She theatrically shrugged her shoulders, took one last look at the garbage on the floor and walked out of the camp without looking back.

* * * * *

Jake turned his attention on Hugh. He sneered down at the cowering lump of crap on the floor and considered pounding the guy into Silly Putty. "Now, buster, are you going to tell me who hired you, or do I have to beat it out of you? And, believe me, nothing is going to give me more pleasure in this life than beating you to a bloody pulp."

Hugh continued to whimper on the floor. Drool clung to his lip, and he sniffed loudly. "I can't tell you. He'll have me killed."

"No problem, but he may not have to go to the bother. I'm just as likely to do it for him. Do you think the police are going to care that I killed you in a skirmish to save Liz? Especially when they find out that you're a killer for hire?" Jake forced a cynical laugh. "I don't think so."

Fists balled tight, he truly had to stop himself from doing bodily harm right now. The guy deserved it like no one he'd ever met.

"No. I'll tell." The big, bad hit man crumpled before his eyes. It was always the meanest and dirtiest who couldn't take what they'd dished out to others.

"Spill it, before I rearrange your face with my steel-toed hiking boot," Jake growled. "Who hired you?"

* * * * *

Liz listened outside the cabin door and dared a glance inside.

"Vince M. from Toronto. I don't know his last name. It was part of our agreement." Hugh shouted the name as if getting rid of it could save him from being beaten.

"Is he Liz's real father?" Again, his fist came close to Hugh's face.

"No... I don't know!" Hugh cringed away like a sniveling dog.

"You dirty son of a..." Jake punched Hugh in the nose, making him howl like a banshee. Jake's muscles shook from the exertion of holding himself back from doing further punishment. Hugh had to believe he was serious, so a well-aimed punch had been necessary.

"You said you wouldn't hurt me if I told," he wailed insipidly.

"Who is he then?"

"Just some guy who wanted her snuffed. I don't ask too many questions. It's not good for business."

"Why did you say it was her father then?"

"I..." Hugh looked at Jake wide-eyed. "If I tell you the truth, you'll hit me again."

"Tell me the truth and I might not hit you again!" he ground out, sweat dripping from his forehead mixing with dried blood. His head pounded like a riveting machine inside his skull was trying its damnedest to get out.

"I heard the guy who hired me talking like he knew her real father."

"When?"

"When he hired me. We met face-to-face at a pub. I didn't get to see his face because he wore a disguise. I'd arrived early and had caught him on the phone before he realized who I was."

Jake raised his fist higher.

Hugh cringed. "I swear, it's the truth. That's all I know."

Jake reached down and jacked him up by the back of his pants.

Hugh shrieked as his pants rode up on him while Jake frog-walked him to the vehicle and shoved him into the back seat. He climbed into the driver's seat next to Liz, who waited in the passenger seat.

Liz glanced back uncomfortably at Hugh, then at Jake. "Where are we going?"

"I guess back to Fredericton."

"What if we go to Toronto?" Liz suggested.

Hugh started to wail. "Don't take me to Toronto, you bastards. I'm not going there."

Jake grinned. "I see your point. How'd you know?"

"He was talking in his drunken stupor back in the cabin. He mumbled 'Toronto' several times. I have the feeling that's where he was taking me, even though he said he planned to take me back to Bangor."

"Toronto it is, then."

"Please, drop me off at a police station in New Brunswick. Don't leave me taped up for that long. I just drank two bottles of booze. I've got to piss."

"Watch your language," Jake snapped. "There's a lady present."

Hugh snorted. "Well, whether there is or isn't, I've got to go."

"Where's that chloroform?" Jake growled angrily but winked at Liz when he saw her horrified expression.

"Don't chloroform me. I'll hold it."

"You'd better, because I'm not going to listen to you bellyaching back there. I don't know how much chloroform to use, either." He looked sideways at Liz. "Can't too much be dangerous?" He winked at her again.

"Yes, it damned well is dangerous," Hugh shouted.

"Yeah, well, we'll play it by ear. If he gets noisy, we'll do it anyway," he said to Liz. "I don't know about you, but I've just about had it up to here today." He ran his index finger across his throat and spoke in his gruffest voice.

Not another peep came from the back seat. Half an hour down the road, they stopped, and Jake let Hugh relieve himself. Torture wasn't Jake's style.

It was daylight again when they finally reached the city traffic of Toronto. Even though they tried the whole trip, Hugh wouldn't tell them anything else, so they decided to get rid of him as soon as possible. They'd drop him off at the cop shop then do some research of their own.

Jake didn't want to leave her alone with him again, so he pulled the van up to the front door of the police station. "I'll keep our guest under wraps while you go get a cop, okay?"

Without saying a word, she nodded and hopped out, quickly making her way to the front door of the station. He admired the hell out of her. She was a strong woman. After all she'd gone through, she still managed to do whatever had to be done.

* * * * *

Goose bumps rose on her arms while she crossed the sidewalk and climbed the steps to the bland gray brick building. A police officer narrowed his gaze on her from behind his protective Plexiglas window. "Are you all right? Do you need some help?"

She'd forgotten about the bruises on her face and her state of attire. No wonder the officer was instantly concerned. "I'm Liz Davis." He obviously recognized her name right away. Apparently, the news of her disappearance had spread across Canada as well as the US.

"Officer, I don't know what you think you know about me, but I've been abducted by a man who has been trying to kill me. He's the person who blew up my house in Maine. My neighbor rescued me."

The officer frowned at her. "That's not what the papers are saying," he said.

"My friend and I have got the man who kidnapped me. He's tied up in the car outside." She pointed in the direction of the doors.

The officer sat straighter and actually looked startled before he leaned over the desk so he could see through the front doors.

"Chief Hanlon from Bangor knows my case. Maybe you could phone him?"

"Yes, ma'am. I'll do that."

He immediately called for backup and sent an officer out to Jake before he dialed the Bangor Police Department's number that Liz had given him. She'd called it enough times during her random incidents that she knew it by heart. After papers arrived by fax from Chief Hanlon, there was no question Hugh had to be arrested. Apparently, the cops were already aware of Hugh's criminal history, and they suspected he had been on the run after Liz's place blew.

By the time they had Hugh safely incarcerated and their stories taken down, she and Jake had been up for over twenty-four hours. It didn't matter that it was noon, they badly needed sleep.

"Look, officer," Jake said, motioning his head toward Liz. "She's been through hell the last few weeks. Do you think we could come back tomorrow to finish this up? We've been driving for hours and we're exhausted."

The officer considered that for a moment. "Sure, tomorrow will work. By then we should be ready to ask a few more questions."

Liz sighed and shrugged her shoulders. "I guess it'll have to be the nearest hotel?"

Jake wrapped an arm around her shoulder, and they started for the main door. Jake stopped suddenly. "I'll be right back." He went back to the officer at the desk. They talked in low whispers. The officer looked up at her twice, so she knew that they were talking about her. Finally, Jake nodded and said, "See you tomorrow."

"What was all that about?"

"Nothing important," he said.

"Then why was the officer looking at me several times while you were talking? You were obviously discussing me. Don't you think I deserve to be let in on the big secret?"

He kissed her fully on the lips, shocking her into silence. "It's nothing for you to worry about," he answered her gently. "I just asked about hotels."

The nearest hotel appeared expensive. Liz got out of the car and looked up at the elaborate exterior. "Can we afford this?"

"We can." He smiled at her, probably because she'd used the royal "we." She had no money.

Signing in didn't take long. They took the elevator to the third floor and found the room. Jake opened the door, and she looked inside. "Hey, wait, there's no door between our rooms." She'd been wandering around the lobby while he booked the rooms. She assumed they'd have adjoining suites.

* * * * *

Jake looked up and down the hall then pulled her inside and shut the door. "We're sharing this room."

She put her hands on her hips and frowned. "Sorry, I shouldn't have expected you to pay for two rooms. This hotel is obviously expensive. Why don't we go somewhere else?"

He pulled her to the side of the bed, where she sat down unceremoniously beside him, her fatigue evident. "I'm not going to leave you alone after the day you've had. What type of a friend would I be then? And don't worry, I can afford this room." He grinned at her. "For one night at least."

Fatigue obviously clawed at her, and he doubted she could make the move to another hotel, even if she insisted on it. "Why don't you have a nice hot bath?" he said. She had dirt on her face and hands from being dragged across the forest floor. It would probably take a good soak to get it all off.

He leaned toward her, and for a very long moment, the need to kiss her overwhelmed him.

He took a deep breath, stood and helped her to her feet. He put both hands on her shoulders and turned her toward the bathroom. "See? You're so tired you can hardly keep your eyes open, but you'll still feel better even if you only have a quick shower."

He was right. She felt like she'd been rolling in the mud. She'd gotten some pretty odd looks from people in the lobby. Funny, how being alive after what had happened to her made her feel differently about how she looked all covered in dirt. So what if they misinterpreted the cause for the dirt? That was their problem.

Hot water and lots of smelly soap would be the perfect balm to her sore body. She might have showered longer if she hadn't been so bone tired. Wrapped in a towel from the hotel, she made for the king-size bed with a European pillow top and down comforter.

Jake waited on the edge of the bed. He stood when she came out of the bathroom.

"I want to thank you," she started, but he held up a hand.

"We have lots to talk about, but let's hold that off until later. We both need sleep." He pulled back the covers and waited for her to crawl in.

"Where are you going to sleep?" she asked, planning to remove the damp towel after she got under the covers, and even though the bed was king-size didn't mean she'd share while she was naked.

"On the settee over there, but I'm going to shower first. Will that keep you awake?" he asked.

She shook her head. She didn't think a typhoon would keep her awake at this point. The covers came over her shoulders, and he tucked them under her chin.

She smiled at him. How would she ever thank him for all that he'd done? She'd think of something. With her eyes already starting to close, she said, "I don't understand why some woman hasn't snapped you up."

"Yeah, yeah. Ada says that, too," he growled in a humorous tone. "Go to sleep."

Chapter Twelve

At six that evening Liz got dressed and made coffee in the hotel room. A few solid hours of sleep had helped a great deal, and she felt much better.

She needed a change of clothing in the worst way and hated putting her dirty things back on.

"You okay?" Jake asked.

Focusing on a seascape print on the wall had helped her hold back the floodgate of emotions threatening to break through. She chewed on her lip for a moment, giving herself time to regain some composure.

"Just realizing I've lost everything. I have no home to go back to. I've never really taken the time to think about that. I was too busy running for my life."

He shook his head and leaned against the wall, facing her. "No matter what happened in the past, look at how you've gotten through it."

Touching her stained jeans, she said, "I hate to ask, but can you lend me a few more dollars so I can buy some clothes before we go back to the police station?"

"Of course. When do you want to go?"

"Before dinner maybe? I can manage the way people look at me in public for a little while longer."

"I'm sure that happens to you all the time."

She frowned at him quizzically. "I'm sorry?"

"Men always look at pretty women." He suddenly looked uncomfortable and kept his thoughts to himself for the next while.

When they found a chain store, she bought two new pairs of jeans, two tops, a nightgown, and underwear. They'd have to do her until she got home. She'd tried to get money from the bank machine, but her accounts had been locked. Most likely due to her so-called demise. Still exhausted, she fell asleep almost as soon as she got back to the room.

When it was time to go to the police station the next day, she felt like running again. That wouldn't help with the reality of her situation. Her father had taught her to be stronger than that. Besides, she needed to know why.

She looked out of their hotel room and peered across the landscape of the city. "It seems brighter today, doesn't it?" she said, forcing some optimism into her voice.

Jake joined her at the window. He smelled delicious, and for that reason, she kept her attention away from him and on the city. As much as she'd tried to deny her feelings, she'd been attracted to him since day one. Yeah, he'd kissed her twice, but that didn't mean he felt anything for her. And why would he? She'd been nothing but trouble.

"Much brighter," he said, but his expression didn't lighten. He seemed preoccupied. In fact, he had been that way since they'd arrived here. Hugh was in jail. Shouldn't that count for something? Maybe he wanted to go home.

"Ready to go?" he asked.

She nodded reluctantly. "We'll probably be at the police station for hours today."

"Most likely," he said, aiming a forced smile in her direction. She hated putting him in this position.

She reached out and made contact with Jake, squeezing his hand. It surprised her when he reciprocated by picking up her hand and kissing the inside of her wrist.

At a loss for words, she felt a blush heat her face. What did it mean? Hey, if you're interested in me, I'm interested in you, too? She'd probably put too much into his actions. He'd never said he was doing anything other than helping her—end of story.

They stepped outside into the bright morning sunlight. "Do we really have to go to that awful police station this morning?" she asked.

"Unfortunately, you know we do." He led her to the car and waited for her to buckle herself in. "Liz?"

"Yes?" He'd seemed overly preoccupied this morning.

"You've been exceptionally strong throughout this whole thing."

She frowned. Was this the big kiss-off? Already?

"You still need some of that strength I've seen from day one," he said.

She stiffened her back. "What do you mean?"

"Even though Hugh is in jail, he is only a hired hit man. Whoever this Vince M. is hired Hugh. He is the one who wants you dead."

"Oh crap! Do you think he'll hire someone else when he finds out Hugh failed? I was so happy to be out of danger. I'd completely blocked out the hit man factor."

Jake's mouth pursed and he started the car. His hands clamped tight on the steering wheel.

"Funny, I thought you were going to tell me you had to go home and I'd be on my own. That was my worst fear." She didn't mean to bare her soul to him, but the truth was out now. He might as well know how she felt, and it would give him the opening he might need to leave.

He took a long breath. "I'm not going to leave you. I'm going to help you through this to the end."

She sagged in her seat. Tears threatened to break the impenetrable dam she'd erected. "One ray of sunshine in this dark hole that has become my life," she croaked out.

"I promise not to leave until you're safe," he said.

"Jake. That's too much for you to offer. Who knows how long this could go on?"

"One way or another, I plan to see you through this," he said adamantly.

She had to face reality. This thing could go on for months…years. Her stomach felt like lead. She'd never hold him to his promise.

With her mood much darker, she found herself back at the police station and being led down a long, dingy corridor to a room with a rectangular table and several chairs around it.

Liz entered first. She spotted the other woman instantly. "Maggie! Oh Maggie!" She ran to her friend and wrapped her arms around the woman.

Maggie's eyes looked red from crying. She hugged Liz then sobbed into her shoulder. "Liz, my poor baby. Are you all right? I would never have been able to forgive myself if Hugh had killed you."

Liz sat on the hard wooden chair next to Maggie's and held her hands. "Hugh told me you were dead," she said, brushing away the tears of happiness at finding Maggie alive.

"He tried, but I got out of your house before it blew. The police made it look like he'd killed me in order to protect me from him."

"Why are you here now?" Liz asked.

"I couldn't stay away. I had to see you," she said. "And I had to tell my side of the story to make sure Hugh is extradited and goes to jail for a very long time."

"Did you know he was trying to kill me?" Liz asked. She looked across at Jake for support. He hovered near her protectively.

Maggie sniffed into her tissue. "No, dear. I didn't know. I was in the garage one morning and saw the propane heater and things that he used in your house. They didn't mean that much to me then. I had no idea what he was up to until he shoved me down your basement stairs and locked the door." Her eyes got big, then squinted up as tears filled them again. "He wanted me to be blown up with the house, but I got out through the basement window behind the furnace just one time. Hugh didn't notice that window or I'd probably be dead right now. You wouldn't believe the weapons and horrible things that man had hidden in the garage. The FBI found them after your house blew up and I'd reported my near-death experience."

A faraway expression crossed her face. "I married the man, and I didn't even suspect."

"Maggie, I'm so sorry."

"At first I didn't want to believe it, you know. I was married to the man for five years. I knew he was a cold, hard man with a mean streak. But I didn't know he was a murderer." Tears started running down her face again and plopping onto her white sweater.

Liz squeezed Maggie's hands to give her comfort.

The door opened, and a tall, thin man entered wearing an impeccable suit. His salt-and-pepper hair was perfectly clipped, and his shoes shone like he'd spit polished them just before he walked into the room. He seemed out of place in a police station. He held out his hand to Jake. "Good day, I'm Lieutenant Bourgeois, the investigating detective on this case." He walked across the room and shook Liz's hand next.

She found his cologne strong. She imagined it was also expensive.

Obviously, he'd already met Maggie. He tipped his head in her direction, seemingly unwilling to be affected by her state of remorse. Liz put her arm protectively around Maggie's shaking shoulders.

"I understand that Mr. Cranston gave up the name of the person who hired him while in your presence?" He looked at Liz.

"He did," Jake said, stepping forward. "Sort of."

The detective gave him a curt nod. "Mr. Johnston, please have a seat next to Miss Davis," he said, then sat across the table from them. "Unfortunately, Mr. Cranston is denying that he gave you anyone's name. He's completely clammed up."

Why wasn't she surprised? She looked for Maggie's reaction. She felt so sorry for her friend. It must be devastating to know they were talking about the man she'd married. Maggie dabbed at her eyes with a tissue.

"Where does that leave us?" Liz asked.

Detective Bourgeois began to tap his pen against the table, an irritating staccato sound that made Liz edgy.

"We will investigate but there's very little to go on other than your testimony. We don't even have the name of his supposed client," he said in a strong French accent. "We have enough incriminating evidence against Mr. Cranston, though. The FBI will be arriving shortly to take him back to Bangor. And since his wife has allowed the authorities to go through the garage and confiscate his things, there's plenty of evidence against him."

"Without proof that Vince M. is connected, we can't do much about him, other than perform a superficial investigation. Mr. Cranston has denied any connection to Vince M. and told us that he gave you the false name under duress just so you would stop beating him. His face is very bruised." He gave Jake an inquiring look.

Jake let out an angry sound. "That bastard! Does that mean you can't find out why this unknown person wants Liz dead?" Jake leaned forward against the table and looked directly into Lt. Bourgeois' face.

"If there really is someone who wants Miss Davis dead—we'll do what we can within the parameters of the law. It might take awhile to get a warrant, because we have to have an actual name first."

"How long are we talking?" Jake asked.

Lt. Bourgeois grimaced. "Asking for a warrant without just cause makes things a little trickier, especially since Cranston won't back up your statement. It could be months. Even if we knew who Vince M. was."

Liz caught Jake's hopeless expression.

Maggie sniffed and spoke up. "To think I'm married to a hit man. Why would he go after Liz? It doesn't make sense to me."

Join the club, Liz thought.

The detective perused everyone in the room before he spoke. "I'm sorry, Mrs. Cranston, but there's no doubt in my mind that he is a hit man. According to the reports from Bangor, they found many things in the garage that incriminated him. He had the appropriate equipment. Very sophisticated listening devices, powerful weaponry, tools of the trade and some DNA evidence. As a matter of fact, we found a tracking device in his van. I suggest you go through Ms. Davis' things to find out if she'd been tagged." He looked at Liz. "He probably has a tracking device somewhere in your things, possibly your purse. Most women take their purses with them everywhere."

"My purse was blown up in my car." She gave him a bewildered look. "That certainly explains how he found me so quickly in New Brunswick, though." She looked at Jake. "He knew where I was the whole time."

Lt. Bourgeois nodded. "Would you mind if we check your clothing?"

Was he going to frisk her? "My old clothes are in the dumpster behind the hotel," she said.

"Which hotel?"

She told him, and he picked up a phone and spoke quickly. He gave her orders to retrieve Liz's clothes from behind the hotel.

"Tell me about your car blowing up," he said and leaned against his fingers tented on the table.

While they recounted what had happened in Fredericton for what felt like hours, the officer returned with Liz's clothes. The policewoman held a small disk-like object that looked like a watch battery with protruding wires inside a plastic evidence bag. Lt. Bourgeois took it from her and held it up between his thumb and forefinger and looked it over. "State-of-the-art tracking devices like this aren't cheap." He turned to the detective. "Any fingerprints?"

She nodded. "Just one print, and it belongs to Cranston."

"Good," Bourgeois said and stood. It appeared their meeting was over. "You can go for now. I'll be in touch once I have more information for you." He crossed the room and opened the door, turning and eyeing each of them in turn. "Ms. Davis please leave your contact information with the detective before you go. Mrs. Cranston, you're free to go home, if you wish. We already have your information, and we'll contact you if we need you further. It's unlikely we will, since your husband will be escorted back to Maine very shortly."

The three of them exited the building. They stopped at the bottom of the steps. "That's it?" Liz kicked a pebble on the sidewalk and wondered where it had come from in a concrete city.

Maggie had left with them and they stood outside the police department on the sidewalk. "I guess I don't have much choice, I have to go home for now," she said. She reached over and gave Liz a peck on the cheek. "Keep in contact with me, dear. Tell me what's happening? By the way, I've had my phone fixed if you've been trying to contact me."

"I certainly will," Liz said. "Listen, may I stay with you for a bit when I come home?"

Maggie's distraught face lit up. "I'll be thrilled to have you stay with me any time, dear."

Liz made a face. "As soon as we get this case figured out."

The second she was out of sight, Jake turned on her. "You don't really want to stay with her, do you?"

Liz frowned at him. "It's not Maggie who did this to me."

He looked like he didn't believe that. "Okay, let's forget about that for now. We've got to find another place to stay for a few days."

They walked along the sidewalk, going nowhere in particular. "When you talked to the policeman last night, you told him you thought I was still in jeopardy, didn't you?"

"Yes, I didn't want to upset you. At least you got one good night's sleep before being reminded of the grim reality."

She furrowed her brow. "Yet, we're openly walking along the sidewalk?"

"This is pure supposition on my part, but I've been thinking. If someone hired Hugh, and I believe it really is this Vince M. I don't think he pulled that name out of his...out of the air."

Her eyebrows rose, and she grinned at him.

"For now, whoever he is, he can't possibly know about Hugh being arrested."

"I hope you're right," she said in a whisper.

"Let's find another hotel since we have to stay here for a few more days. I don't know about you, but I could use a few minutes of vegging out," Jake said.

"Me, too."

* * * * *

Jake hoped he hadn't spoiled his chances with her by treating her like she was crazy when she tried to tell him someone was trying to kill her. He wouldn't blame her if that fact remained a wedge between them. He'd been blind and stupid.

He stared blankly at the television screen while Liz showered that night. He couldn't stop thinking about her. About those gorgeous dark brown eyes and blond hair that felt like brushed silk under his fingers. Her tempting bod and that stubborn way she'd look at him when she was afraid. The sweet floral scent of her. Damn it, the thought of losing her was unthinkable.

With that in mind, he figured they shouldn't stay in one hotel for too long. It might be better if they moved around. For tonight, this hotel had good enough security and was more affordable than the last. And this time they had two double beds.

Even though it was likely Vince M. didn't know Hugh Cranston was in jail, they'd be smart to lie low for a couple of days until the police got a lead on the man. If they got a lead.

She came out of the shower smelling like heaven and looking like a squeaky-clean angel. Wearing a terry housecoat supplied by the hotel, she happily lathered hand cream onto her legs, barely noticing that he watched her with rapt attention.

He liked the way her expression changed when she caught him staring at her. He didn't try to hide the desire that showed on his face. He couldn't have, even if he'd wanted to.

And right now, he needed to put some distance between them, because he was too close to pulling her into his arms. "I'm going to get some water at the machine down the hall," he said. "I'll be right back."

She nodded and started flipping channels. When he returned, they both drank a nice cold bottle of water, and he suggested they watch a movie. She sat on the bed beside him. She fell asleep partway through, her head on his arm.

He tried to get comfortable without waking her. From now on, he'd have to make sure he didn't touch her, because every time he did, it was like a slow, steady volcanic reaction building in him, until he wanted more and more.

* * * * *

Liz woke slowly to the delicious scent of Jake. His beating heart against her ear quickened as if he realized her secret desire. She adjusted herself and his arm gently folded her closer. She lifted her head and he looked down at her. His gaze heated her in a tantalizing flush. His head tipped and he kissed her tentatively. Exploring at first.

Pressing herself against him in acceptance, she felt herself swirling into a delicious cocoon of excitement. Until, he hungrily slipped off her nightgown and then his own clothes while his warm, moist tongue began a sensual exploration of her body.

Almost painfully aware of her own breathlessness and heated excitement, she took infinite pleasure in each sensation he aroused within her. Sensation after sensation, he led her to the brink of awareness and need.

He slowly worked his way back to her mouth where he kissed her deeply again. His hands caressed her, molded her and brought her to the exquisite certainty of his touch. He was a master at the ability to drive her extremely close to the edge over and over again before he'd slow the pace, give her time to defuse just long enough before he'd begin all over again. Tantalizing, driving her need to contemplate begging for satisfaction. His mouth covered hers with kisses so hot, so intimate and probing she nearly forgot what his hands were doing to her. Almost!

They didn't speak. Too intent on the pleasures they were eliciting, they continued until she'd forgotten all of her fears and troubles. This unending desire—the need for completion had consumed her. She explored his firm muscles, which were suddenly as moist as she'd become. Nearly robbed of breath now, there was no turning back. Pleasure had become paramount.

Pleasure she'd elicited in him as well, if his ragged breathing meant anything. After which he molded himself against her, sending her lust into overdrive. They'd become as intertwined in body as in soul. There was nothing else but hot body against hot body. Strength against softness. Finally with his mouth adoring her, his body paying homage to her, he took her over the edge to a searing exquisite finale and then sweetness that she'd never experienced before. Total and complete ecstasy.

Chapter Thirteen

Liz woke first. Even before she opened her eyes, she felt his skin against her cheek and smelled his clean scent. One of her arms stretched over him with her hand on his bare, taut stomach.

He stirred and turned onto his side, talking in his sleep as he settled himself.

No matter what happened in the future, she never wanted to forget this moment. Forget last night.

His face was darkened by stubble, his long eyelashes practically touching his cheeks, his arms so strong and at the same time gentle.

Somehow, she managed to get washed and dressed without waking him. She left the room with barely a click of the lock. After last night, she thought he'd appreciate a hearty breakfast.

The restaurant had just opened, and freshly brewing coffee scented the air. The place was virtually empty. She ordered breakfast to go and had it billed to the room. Crossing the center of the lobby with the food in two brown paper bags, she pushed the elevator button and stared absently at the shiny chrome doors while the changing LED numbers indicated floors.

The elevator door opened with Jake inside.

"What are you doing?" he whispered, holding the elevator door for her to enter. "Do you have a death wish?"

"Why are you saying that?"

Dressed only in jeans, his hair still tousled from sleep, he looked extremely agitated. "I'm sorry. I shouldn't have jumped at you. It's just—you scared the spit out of me."

She stiffened and stepped inside the elevator. "I just went to get our breakfast." She checked the paper bag that had their coffee in it, wondering if she had spilled any of the hot liquid out of the covered paper cups.

He ran a hand through his hair. Still in his bare feet, he hadn't even taken the time to put shoes on before he went looking for her.

"Jake, let's have breakfast and forget about this. I'm fine. Nothing happened."

"Do you remember the last time you went off without me?"

Back in their room, she said, "I can't think about that right now." She started unpacking their breakfast and placing it on the oval table near the window. "I figured I could get us breakfast in the same hotel without risking my life. But if you really think I might not be safe even here—I don't know if I can live like this."

If only she could find Uncle Brody. That would let Jake off the hook.

She reached out tentatively, then pulled her hand back. "Jake, I'm sorry. Really. Thank you for caring."

"The thing is, we've got to stay together on this, Liz. We can't get sloppy again, like we did at that gas stop. Lives depend on it."

She shoved the food at him. "Eat your breakfast before it gets cold," she said.

"I'm sorry that I scared you," he said. "I admit I overreacted."

Not very hungry anymore, she nibbled silently. When she'd gotten up that morning and scurried to the lobby restaurant for the food, she'd been on the edge of feeling happy, but now she could hardly choke down her food.

Since she'd put the bill on his tab, she forced herself to eat a little. Hadn't she already cost him enough, monetarily and time wise?

"Liz," he said, wiping his hands on a paper napkin. "The police called while you were out. Hugh made his one phone call."

She wondered why he stopped in midsentence. "Yes?"

"He didn't call a lawyer."

"Oh." The reality of those words crept through her like a vine with a stranglehold. "Who'd he call?"

"They don't know. They can't legally tap the phone without just cause. They do know he didn't call a lawyer. The guard waiting for him listened in and reported the conversation. He told someone that he'd failed his assignment and if they still wanted him on the job to get him a lawyer."

No wonder Jake had freaked when she'd gone for breakfast. "So, what do we do now? Do the police want to put us under protection?"

He shook his head, his expression serious. Not until there's a direct threat to you."

"But they believe us?"

"Yes. After that phone call, they do, but their hands are tied." He finished his eggs and bacon and tossed his napkin into the garbage can. "We're on our own. Again."

"I see." She mechanically stood. She thought for a moment then turned to him, hands on her hips. "Well, this is ridiculous. You're not at risk if you're not with me. And you have a job to go to. I can't possibly ask you to stay with me any longer."

She wanted to say the exact opposite of every word. She couldn't imagine losing him at this point. But she had to give him the chance to leave so she said, "You've done more for a stranger than most people would. I honestly wouldn't blame you if you had to get back to your job."

* * * * *

Jake watched her throw away the food. He'd listened to her words. Stranger? A stranger. Did she mean that? Her words stung, and they made the impact she obviously wanted them to. Too bad, because he wasn't about to give up on her.

He crossed to the window and looked at the parking lot below. The last three years he'd dated on again, off again. None of the women were ever in his life long term, and that's the way he liked it. Liz needed more from him than anyone he'd ever known, not exactly what he thought he wanted in a woman. What made him think he was what she needed? Given everything that had happened since he first met her, the characteristics of a knight in shining armor would suit her needs nicely. He didn't exactly fit those needs. He'd even let her be kidnapped on his watch. No. She needed someone who had it all. Bravery, strength of will, strength of character, and gentleness. Big shoes to fill in order to keep her alive.

And now, on top of everything else he'd done or failed to do, he told her that her life might be in danger again. She reacted by pushing him even further away.

"I'm not leaving you until this thing is over and you're safe," he said.

She planted her arms over her chest and scowled at him. "If you're crazy enough to want to stay with me, that's your problem," she said in an angry tone.

"Good, we're in agreement." Her hissing and scratching wouldn't scare him off.

"I've got to contact my lawyer. Since everyone knows I'm alive now, at least I can get some funds to survive on for the next while, and I did have fire insurance on my home." She made the call to Maine, and her lawyer advised her to meet with a friend of his, a lawyer in Toronto named Bissett. He suggested she might need representation before this thing was over. Her lawyer promised to fill Bissett in on some of her legal details, and he could act as their intermediary until she got home.

She called Bissett. He had a cancellation within an hour, and she and Jake went directly there.

Jake waited in the outer office while she met with the lawyer. When she came out, she had money in her hand. Bissett came out behind her with a wide smile on his face. A slight man with gray hair and hawk-like faded blue eyes looked him over sharply.

"Jake, this is Mr. Bissett," she said.

Jake held out his hand and met the man's firm grip.

"You take good care of Ms. Davis, young man. From what I hear, this gal has been through quite enough."

* * * * *

Liz swallowed hard. Sympathy was the last thing she needed right now. "Thanks, Mr. Bissett," she said, but her words came out shakier than she wanted.

Jake touched the small of her back and ushered her through the door. That simple touch grounded her, made her realize she wasn't alone, and it felt good to know he was there for her.

"My lawyer wired money to hold me over until I get home and get my affairs in order. He seems to think my funds might be tied up for a while yet, but at least I have enough to pay you back."

He held up a hand. "There's no hurry for that, Liz. You might need that money before you get home." He grinned at her, and his blue eyes met hers. How many times had he looked into her eyes and made her feel safe since she'd moved to Fredericton?

She didn't want to admit it, but she was glad she hadn't driven him away. And for some strange reason, he'd promised to stay with her until he knew she was safe. How had she gotten so lucky in the midst of all her troubles?

During a quick trip to a department store, she bought her favorite style of purse, one that slung over her shoulder like a backpack, as well as a small assortment of makeup and lady's toiletries, Jake followed her around the store, keeping a sharp eye on their surroundings.

She started unloading her items at the register. "Hope I didn't forget anything."

Had he noticed her cautiously scanning their surroundings? Still in jeopardy and risking his life, too. Added to that, Jake had taken leave and spent his money to get her to safety. She touched her lips and caught him watching her. She forced a smile. "I don't know how I'll pay you back," she said on a sigh.

"You don't have to pay me back." He sounded offended. "I'm doing this for me as much as for you."

"Really? I don't get it. How could you be doing any of this for yourself?"

"Honestly," he said. "I need to help you solve this." His expression turned dark. "Awhile ago I tried to help someone who trusted me. I suggested she go to a women's shelter. Because of my advice, she ended up badly beaten by her abusive husband. I know this won't take back what happened to her, but I'm not about to let anything happen to you."

His comment disappointed her. She'd wanted a different answer. That he was doing this for her because he adored her. Dream on, chickie! "How is your friend now?"

"She divorced him, even though it took awhile. He got the message eventually and left her alone. And she wasn't upset with me. She said he would have beaten her whether she'd gone to the women's shelter or not. She doesn't blame me, but I blame myself."

Liz nodded, not sure whether she liked being his next project. The person who could assuage his guilty conscience.

Truth was, she was using him, too. Guilt bit into her when she said, "Let's go, then."

Worse, she was developing feelings for him. She thought he liked her, too, but now she knew the truth. He had his own reasons for doing this, not because he cared for her.

After dinner, they pulled up to the hotel and Jake handed his keys to the porter.

This was their third hotel in as many days. Liz stepped inside the room first and looked around. This place was more extravagant than she was used to since she and her family had lived fairly meagerly on her dad's military salary and then pension. "Wow, pretty nice, don't you think?" she said, eyeing the marble floors in the bathroom.

He nodded. "You take the bedroom," he said.

After last night, she thought they might share the bedroom. Unfortunately, since they'd left the police department he'd been disturbed. Most likely because the police weren't able to protect her and he thought he should.

Apparently he had other things on his mind tonight. Like guarding her. "Where will you sleep?"

"Out here on the couch. No one's getting past me tonight."

"I don't think you need to do that," she said. "Surely we're safe here in our room."

She took her cup of tea and sat on the wingback near the window. Sleep edged at her and she let herself drift off.

Awakened by a cotton blanket being placed on top of her, she cracked open her eyes to see Jake backing away from her.

"Thanks for the blanket. Sorry about earlier." Glancing out the window, it surprised her to see the sky had gone from bright blue to black. It had been around three o'clock when she'd dozed off. "What time is it?"

"Ten." He answered, sitting in a chair beside her. "And don't worry about being upset. You have every right to be. Are you hungry?"

"I guess." She rubbed her eyes and rested her face in the palms of her hands.

"I ordered dinner. Do you like chicken Parmesan? It's still warm."

"Not only does it sound wonderful, but it smells wonderful, too." She sat up and sniffed the air appreciatively. "I didn't even hear it being delivered."

"No. You were sound asleep." He held out his hand and helped her off the chair. Touching is nice, she thought.

There was a small round table in the center of the room set formally with a bottle of wine and a flower in the center. Placemats covered the rich pecan finish of the wood.

He poured them each a glass of white wine. She looked worried as he did so. "You didn't buy expensive wine, did you? I'm afraid I'm not a connoisseur, and it might be wasted on me."

He laughed. "Don't worry, it's a bottle we can well afford."

She took a sip of the wine. "Nice."

"It is," he agreed.

After dinner, they sat in side-by-side chairs staring through the huge window that overlooked the sprawling city of Toronto. Lights of the CN Tower flashed in the distance.

She looked at him—at his blue eyes with thick lashes, his sensuous mouth that drew her thoughts away from reality over and over again. She'd like nothing better than to go over there and sit on his lap and melt into his kisses.

But she was a marked woman, and no matter how much she cared about him and wanted to let him know how she felt, she couldn't. She'd only get him killed.

"I think I'll go to bed," she said. The further away from him she stayed, the better at the moment, or her willpower might give out. Maybe it was her imagination, but the way he was looking at her right now sent little spurs of delicious sensations zinging along her nerve endings.

Stretched out in bed, she realized for the first time in ages that her aches and pains seemed almost nonexistent. Of course, she recognized that the wine might have something to do with that. Her eyes had started to close, and maybe she'd fallen asleep, before she felt the presence of someone else in the room. Her heart started to pound, and she grabbed the blankets in tight fists.

Oh God, he's found me.

Chapter Fourteen

She woke early and found that Jake had already ordered room service. She opted for toast and tea. "I woke this morning thinking someone had been in my room last night. After the insidious ways Hugh got into my rental place, I guess I'm still afraid it'll happen again. If not Hugh, then someone else."

"No one got in here last night. If that door had opened I'd have heard it since I slept on the couch two feet away from it."

"Thanks for doing that," she said, really wishing he'd joined her in the bedroom. She didn't blame him for not wanting to continue their intimacy. He probably thought they'd made a mistake. Who'd want to get too close to someone like her? "I wonder if I'll ever feel safe again?"

By his expression, she guessed he'd been remembering their night together, too. She'd like nothing better than to wrap herself in his arms. Except, she'd been thinking last night, and had come to the conclusion that Jake deserved a girlfriend who wasn't being hunted by a killer.

He stood and paced to the window, his expression serious. "Liz, we should try to find out who this Vince guy is ourselves rather than wait for the police to do it. There's not much to go on, and without a last name, the odds are pretty slim they'll make any headway."

She felt a lump settle in her chest. If this didn't work she'd have to go into hiding again. At least without a tracking bug she might have a chance. She bit her lip. "How can we find him if the police can't?"

"I remembered something this morning. A piece of paper fell out of Hugh's pocket in the cabin after he knocked me down. I picked it up and shoved it in my pocket after we scuffled. With everything else going on, I'd completely forgotten about it until now."

"What's on it?"

He dug it out of his pocket and smoothed out the wrinkles. The ink had faded but was obviously a street address in Ontario.

"I think we should check it out. It can't be a coincidence that Vince M. is in this province, too."

"But…" She bit her lip. "That address is miles outside Toronto."

"Wouldn't you rather find out who Vince M. is and why he wants you dead? Waiting for him to find you only gives him the advantage."

She nodded, but her stomach felt tight.

He took her hand and squeezed it. "The sooner we get this thing figured out, the sooner we can get back to our normal lives."

She didn't blame him for wanting his life back. He had a job and a life to lead—without her.

She glanced out he window not really looking at anything. "This isn't getting better, it's just getting worse."

Not understanding what she was trying to tell him, he said, "The cops will try to find him, but they don't have the manpower to put an officer on you. And, like it or not, you can't do this alone. I won't let you do this alone." He grabbed her and pulled her close. His mouth brushed her hair and she buried her face in his chest and inhaled his scent. She was being selfish. She shouldn't let him stay.

"Why Jake? You don't have to do this."

"I know that," he said. With his chin touching the top of her head they both stared out the window. "You know that I care about you. I don't want to leave you alone."

She exhaled. "If anything happened to you, do you know how I'd feel?"

"The same way I'd feel if anything happened to you, perhaps," he pulled her tighter to him. "It really would be better for us to do the pursuing for a change, don't you think? Have the upper hand? This man's probably not going to expect us to come after him," he said.

The prospect scared her witless. But either way she'd be afraid, so she might as well be proactive and afraid. And with Jake at her side she felt braver. "I don't want to be a prisoner of fear. I want to know why this man wants me dead," she said. "I really don't want to get you killed in the process, though."

He ignored that. "I spent most of last night thinking about this. We'll track him down and do some surveillance of our own to find out who he is. If we're lucky we might not even have to come face-to-face with him."

"Sounds reasonable," she said.

"Good." He let go of her and backed away a few steps. "You stay here while I go check out this address."

She grabbed her plastic bag of clothes. "Not likely. I'm coming, too!"

He opened his mouth to argue, saw the look on her face and nodded in reluctant agreement.

First they needed to make their way out of Toronto in noon traffic.

"What's the name of the street?" she asked.

"Buckthorn."

She frowned. Where had she heard that name before?

Liz watched him easily handle the heavy traffic. Obviously, he'd driven in big cities before. He'd never spoken of family, but considering everything they'd gone through, when had he even had time? She felt a little guilty. She'd been so wrapped up in her own troubles, she hadn't asked much about him.

But now she wanted to know. She wanted to know why he was such a good man. She wondered if he had wonderful parents like hers had been.

He'd been fairly quiet their whole trip. He was most likely thinking and rethinking every possible scenario before they found the address.

When Jake pulled the car into the parking lot of a hotel, she said, "Wait a minute. We're supposed to go to the address on the sheet of paper."

"Lets book in first," he said. She knew why. He wanted her to stay here. Not going to happen.

* * * * *

Once inside their room, Jake needed to find a way to persuade her to stay.

She'd been quiet, but once the door shut, she said, "Jake! Did you see the look on that man's face when you said we were Mr. and Mrs. Smith?" She threw herself on the bed and started laughing. "Couldn't you have come up with something more original?"

"There are Smiths in the world, you know." He liked the way she could laugh even though she'd been through hell.

This hotel room was small. The two double beds looked more like super singles. The place looked clean──all they needed for one night.

She giggled again, having what appeared to be a difficult time stopping the laughter. He wondered if she'd be crying next. She was beautiful when she laughed. More beautiful. She lay across the bed, her hair spread out like a halo around her face. He gritted his teeth. He contemplated the dreaded "L" word. He'd finally fallen for a woman and hard. And he didn't know how to tell her, especially considering all she was going through.

"I wonder if Hugh had a designated meeting time," Jake said.

Mentioning Hugh brought her back to reality and wiped the smile off her face in zero seconds flat. He could have kicked himself. He was an idiot.

"You're not leaving me here. I'm going with you."

He plunked onto the bed across from hers. "How'd I know you were going to say that?" He forced a smile and glanced out the window. "The sun's going to set soon. Maybe we should wait to check this place out in the morning? In the light of day."

She nodded, the smile totally gone from her eyes now.

* * * * *

They ate a quick lunch at the fast-food place next door, and when they returned she couldn't settle so she opened the curtains to let in a little light. This building overlooked another hotel and beyond that the sprawling city of Sarnia with Lake Huron in the distance.

She leaned her head against the cool pane of glass and watched the movement of traffic below. "I'm glad we're not up any higher." She looked at the hotel across the way and wondered if any of the people in that hotel knew what it was like to have a hit man chasing them.

"Get out of the window!" Jake grabbed her and threw her roughly onto the bed, just as glass broke and a muffled sound thudded nearby.

"What are you doing?" Liz pushed up off the mattress on her elbows. The first thing she saw was a tiny hole in the glass, then she realized Jake was on the floor and not moving.

"Jake!"

"Liz, honey." He opened his eyes slowly and took a look at his arm.

It was then she saw the blood. She needed to call 911. She started to stand...

"Stay down," he shouted and she dropped to the floor.

"Oh my God, you've been shot!"

Her legs trembled, but she crawled to him. Blood pooled under him and his arm was saturated in blood. "Oh, Jake, don't die. Please, please, don't die."

"Liz, calm down. I'm okay. I was shot in the arm, that's all."

She helped get him more comfortable. Blood stained the carpet.

He pushed himself partially upright against the dresser, and his face turned gray. He looked down at his arm and blanched a little more. "Some bastard shot me. Hurts like hell, but it could've been so much worse." He eyed her seriously. "It could have been you."

Dear heaven, he'd been shot, and he was still thinking about her.

"But how did you know someone was going to shoot?" Liz asked, monitoring his color and pulling up his T-shirt sleeve to see the nasty graze along his arm. "The bullet sliced open the side of your arm." She looked over and saw where it had gone into the dresser. "We have to get the bleeding stopped, though." She crawled to the window, reached up and pulled the curtains closed before crawling back to him.

His color looked better, and he motioned for her to come closer to his face. She moved in, wondering if he wanted to tell her something.

His lips caught hers, and he kissed her long and hard. Good thing she was already on the floor with her hands planted on the rug.

"I suddenly needed that kiss," he said.

"Is that so?" she said, leaning back on her heels and pretending she wasn't monumentally affected. The more time she spent with him, the harder it was to imagine him not being in her life. Her heart lurched. She was in deep trouble, because she cared about him way too much and he didn't feel the same way about her.

"Must've been the shock," he said on pained grin.

"No problem. I needed that kiss, too" she said. "It helped to ground me." She inhaled deeply. What should she do now?

"Is this where I say it's just a flesh wound?" He forced a laugh but ended up gasping when he moved his arm. "Well, besides the fact that it stings like crazy."

"I'll get something to stop the bleeding," she said and crawled into the bathroom where she could safely stand and rummage through the toiletries before grabbing a white hand towel from the rack.

She stepped back into the room without thinking.

"Get down. They still might strafe the room," he said.

She instantly dropped to the floor again, breathing hard. They needed to get out of here but not until she got the bleeding stopped.

She wrapped the towel tightly around his arm and fastened it with safety pins she'd found in a little sewing pack in the bathroom. "This might work."

He gritted his teeth.

"Sorry, I had to make it tight enough," she said. "Now, let's get you comfortable." She propped pillows at his back and leaned him against the dresser again. Next, she cupped his face in her hands and looked into his eyes. "I'm going to call an ambulance."

He dragged his gaze from hers and checked his injury under the towel. "We don't have time for ambulances. And it'd be too easy for whoever did this to track us that way. I'll be fine. I just need a minute."

With her hand still on his face, she sighed. What else could she do?

"If you keep doing that, I'm going to have to kiss you again," he warned.

She pulled her hand away. "You're energetic for someone who's just been shot."

"That because I just had a vision of my future," he said.

She gave him a quizzical look. Did he mean his life flashed before his eyes? His life certainly flashed before her eyes. "What do you mean?"

"I'm going to be okay. Just let me get my bearings for a minute and I'll be fine," he assured.

No matter what he said, she couldn't get past the fact that he needed a doctor. She grabbed the phone.

"Don't call 911," he said. "Honestly, I've had worse injuries on the job."

She very much doubted a meteorologist had had serious injuries like this. She eyed the towel. She expected to see it soaked with blood by now. Thankfully, the bleeding had slowed enough that not much blood had seeped through. She thought about how he'd saved her. "How did you know someone was going to shoot at me?"

"I was sitting on the edge of the bed when I caught a glint of light from one of the windows across the street. At first I thought it was a reflection of the sun on the windows, but then it happened again at precisely the same spot. That's when I dove for you."

"Good instincts for a weatherman," she said. "But I still think you should go to the hospital."

"I'm definitely not going to the hospital for a scratch." He got up off the floor and pulled her with him into the bathroom where they could talk in virtual safety. "I'll report the bullet hole after we leave. Let's get packed quickly."

"I'll pack. You sit on the side of the tub. You're pretty pale."

He looked down at the floor tiles and nodded, obviously unable to argue. "I'll wait here until I'm more steady. Meanwhile, you stay low, okay?"

She quickly grabbed their things and crawled back to the bathroom.

"How'd they find us again?" They looked at each other and repeated the words at the same time. "Another bug?"

He eyed her up and down. "There's one place we haven't checked. The only thing you haven't thrown away," he said. "Your sandals."

She took them off and handed them over. They found a little slit on the back strap of her right sandal. Upon closer inspection, this sandal looked like it'd been tampered with and glued back together again. He grabbed a pen and dug in. It came open, and a tiny silver device fell into his hand.

He got up and flushed it down the toilet. He was still a little pale, but looked stronger now.

"Hugh must have tampered with my shoe when he accessed the house in Fredericton," she said.

Jake eyed her sandal again. "Whoever hired Hugh must not have trusted him and wanted him to bug you in case he lost you."

Fear sliced up her spine and spread like energy sapping tentacles. Even with his hit man in jail, Vince M. was still capable of tracking her and trying to kill her. But why?

"I think we should at least call the detective. We should report what just happened," she said. "Nothing like irrefutable proof that someone is trying to kill you."

"And, yeah, I know what you're thinking," Jake said. "As if Hugh wasn't proof enough."

She nodded in agreement then made the call. Jake leaned closer to the phone in order to listen to what the detective was saying to her.

No surprise that Lt. Bourgeois didn't like their plan. Liz had tried to calm him down in one part of the conversation. In the end, they came to an agreement, with Bourgeois demanding that they think strongly about what they were planning to do. Liz promised to keep him in the loop. He really had no choice in the matter.

"Wow, he really doesn't think we're doing the right thing." She put the phone down gently on the cradle, giving it more attention than was necessary.

* * * * *

"He's probably right." Jake grunted when he moved his arm. He yanked a clean shirt out of his bag that Liz had deposited near him and tried to put it on. His arm felt like a lead weight. He could barely lift it.

She helped him pull the shirt on whether he wanted help or not. "I think we should change our plans for today," she said unfastening the towel on his arm and checking it.

"No way. They probably think they've got us pinned down. They won't expect us to come looking for them."

She'd been in the process of wringing out the bloody towel in order to reapply it to his wound. Her eyes widened at his comment. "I don't think that's a good idea, given what just happened."

"We're only checking the address," he said. "If we can get a full name we can give it to the cops."

Worry lines formed on her forehead while she chewed the edge of her lip. By now he knew her well enough to figure that she was probably trying to devise a plan to change his mind. "We need to do this, Liz. You can't keep looking over your shoulder. Someone has to be proactive before you get shot."

"I'm going with you, too. And I can be as stubborn as you can, so don't even think you can make me stay behind."

He shrugged his shoulders then wished he hadn't. "I'd like to say I don't agree and demand that you stay somewhere safe, but I know that you won't listen to me."

Within ten minutes they pulled up to a curb opposite a multimillion-dollar mansion on a cul de sac filled with other million-dollar homes. The address led them to an executive home in the suburbs of the city.

"Stay in the car. I'm going to ring the doorbell. I can pretend I'm peddling something. Maybe I can get a last name." He squeezed her fingers gently.

Her liquid brown eyes stared into his, and without thinking, he reached over and caressed the back of her neck while he pulled her closer. His mouth found hers, and they kissed until the tension in her muscles lessened and her lips became fully compliant.

"Promise me you'll wait here. Please!"

She nodded, but it was reluctantly. After he stepped out of the car, he looked back several times to make sure she had stayed put. So far, so good.

He figured with a house as large as this one, Vince M. probably had servants. It wasn't likely that the guy would be the person answering the door. He might be able to weasel a last name out of an employee. That's as far as he would go.

The doorbell rang Westminster Abbey chimes. He heard footsteps coming. He stepped to the side just in case it was someone carrying a weapon. He might be a little gun-shy right now.

When the door opened, a thick-necked thug stood inside the doorway.

"I'd like to speak to Mr. Mu...Mu...," Jake said, pretending to stutter. In his experience, people always rushed to fill in words whenever someone stuttered.

"Mossman. He expecting you?" the man asked.

"Mossman? Oh, sorry wrong address."

The guy's eyes narrowed. "Not likely the wrong address. You're coming inside."

Jake started to back away and noticed something in the guy's pocket that looked very much like a gun.

"You want Mr. Mossman?" the man said. "You get to see Mr. Mossman."

"No, really. It's just the wrong address," Jake said.

"Yeah? Not likely, bud. Move…"

Jake reluctantly entered without a backward glance that might give Liz's position away. He probably should have considered this scenario.

Trying to figure out a way to make a break for it, he spotted a fully decked-out dining room that gleamed in rich dark wood, visible through huge glass doors lined with gold paint. No other way out.

With the kind of money this guy obviously had, Jake wondered how Liz could possibly be a problem for this man.

The man led Jake to a door behind a spiral staircase. He opened the door and pushed Jake inside. Jake's every muscle was on alert, every instinct ready for whatever happened.

Mossman sat behind an ornate mahogany desk. He was talking on the phone, and he waved Jake into the room without turning to see who it was.

Jake's eyes narrowed. He examined the room quickly while he stood, legs spread apart, waiting for Mossman's reaction to him. He had a full head of thick black hair. He wasn't tall, but he was fairly ruggedly built. Jake wouldn't have a hope against two of them, not to mention his injured arm.

"Hugh, you've failed me. You didn't complete our agreement."

Shouting came through the phone line.

"Yeah, well as far as I'm concerned you can rot in prison, you have nothing on me," he said finally, smashing the phone down before turning and looking at Jake.

"Who's this?" he growled.

"Says he came to the wrong house," the thug said.

"Did he now?" Vince eyed Jake. "Tell the truth. Why are you here?"

Mossman had a long, aquiline nose and dark olive skin. Jake guessed he might be Greek.

In his open desk drawer—a gun. Crap. He had a gun in there, and he looked like he'd be more than capable of using it.

"Wallet?"

The thug stuck his hand into Jake's pocket, hauled out his wallet and passed it to Mossman.

"Hey!" Jake said, not expecting to be able to stop the big guy.

Mossman opened the wallet and took out his driver's license. "Well, well, if it isn't the pain in the ass Jake Johnston, interfering neighbor. You've got a hell of a nerve coming here, don't you?" He smiled in realization at the little droplets of blood that he suddenly noticed on Jake's shirtsleeve.

Mossman narrowed his gaze on the thug. "Bert, you said you got him through the chest. Apparently you only winged him!"

Bert swallowed loudly. "I thought I did, sir."

"God damn it! Good help is hard to find. Make yourself scarce right now or I'll shoot you myself," he said to his henchman.

"If that's what you want, boss," Bert said, sounding utterly dejected.

"No wait. I'll give you one more chance. Go handle those preparations we discussed earlier. I can manage this punk," Mossman said, baring uneven teeth at the underling who'd failed him. "And don't fuck up this time!"

Bert grumbled something under his breath in Jake's direction, and left in seconds.

"Why are you trying to have Liz killed?" Jake asked. He had nothing to lose now because there was no way Mossman would to let him leave this place under his own steam.

"Wouldn't you like to know?"

"Not only would I like to know, but you're going to tell me." Jake stepped toward him. He had no idea how he'd carry out his threat. But at least Mossman was alone, and it was one against one right now.

Mossman made a grab for the drawer, and Jake dove across the desk, knocking him backward onto the floor. He punched the idiot hard and sent his head back against the hardwood floor.

Jake raised his fist to punch again, but Mossman reached up and dug his nails into the wound. He cursed. Pain burst forth in the form of bright flashes of light behind his eyes, and he fell sideways, hanging on to his arm.

Mossman's girth was a disadvantage for him, luckily. He tried to get up before Jake could, but Jake was quicker.

He went for his desk drawer again.

"You're going down. The police in Toronto know all about you. Cranston is still in jail, and you and I both know he'll talk before he goes to prison. He's not that strong. He just likes to hurt people for money…but when it comes to himself?" Jake shrugged and grinned. "The truth will come out then."

Unfortunately, along with the searing, burning pain in the wound, his arm had started bleeding again.

"You don't know who you're dealing with, punk! You're going to be sorry you came into my house."

"I'll ask it again. Why are you trying to kill Liz?" Jake raised his fist to punch Mossman's face.

"Jake, are you all right?" Jake jerked his head around to see Liz standing in the doorway with an Asian servant.

Unfortunately, the distraction cost him. Mossman kicked out and knocked Jake off his feet, sending another raft of spiking pain through his arm when he hit the floor.

Before he could shout for her to stop, Liz sidestepped the servant and surged forward when Mossman jumped up and went for his desk again.

Somehow she managed to beat him to it. She pulled the silver gun out of the drawer and pointed it at Mossman. "Is this what you were looking for?"

"You wouldn't use that thing on a person," he ground out. "Besides, it's just for show," he said and edged closer to her.

"Liz, don't shoot him," Jake said. "We'll never find out why he hired a hit man if you do that."

"Maybe it won't matter if he's dead," she said angrily.

* * * * *

Her hands shook visibly. She had no intention of shooting anyone. She just wanted to scare him into believing that she could do it if she had to, at least until Jake got back on his feet. Besides, she'd cost Jake's control over the situation and now she had to fix it.

Mossman's gaze narrowed on her. "Watch it, bitch. That gun's got a hair trigger."

Jake scrambled to his feet, blood dripping in three streaks down his arm. "Jake, your arm is bleeding again."

She shouldn't have let herself be distracted, because Mossman took advantage of the distraction and knocked the gun out of her hand. Before she or Jake could grab the gun again, Mossman had pushed past Jake and escaped down the hall toward the back of the house.

Jake took off after him, shouting back to Liz as he went. "Stay put!"

She grabbed the gun again while the servant remained frozen in the doorway of the den with his mouth hanging open.

"Stay right where you are," she told the man, just to be on the safe side. She didn't want him calling for backup. Meanwhile, she sat in the chair behind the desk so she could prop her arms and wait for Jake to return.

More scuffling erupted at the back of the house. Something smashed. As much as Liz wanted to go, she stayed put this time. No way would she put Jake at risk again.

The servant started to slowly edge out of the doorway.

"Stay there or you'll be sorry," she said in the most authoritative voice she'd ever managed while she waved the gun without actually pointing it at him. Hair trigger meant she might shoot the man by accident. While she didn't want that to happen, no way could she give him the chance of helping his boss if that's what he had in mind.

He bowed in her direction several times with his hands held tightly in front of him. He mumbled to himself in Mandarin while he pressed himself against the wall and most likely waited for her to do something stupid. She hoped he wasn't right about that. She didn't plan to do anything else that would compromise Jake's safety.

Seconds turned into minutes that felt like hours. Should she call the cops? She strained to hear anything coming from the back of the house. Her hand got tired of holding the heavy gun while she kept her attention on the man across the room.

At the sound of footsteps approaching the den, she lifted the gun into the air once more. The man she'd held captive started mumbling wildly in Mandarin again.

"Shhh!" she said, frowning at him and trying to look more badass than she'd ever be in real life.

He closed his eyes and pressed his palms together and looked up to heaven. She wondered if he had any idea what kind of a monster he worked for, especially if he thought she was scary.

The sound of footsteps drew nearer. Her throat dried out, her head started to buzz. She took a deep breath. Please let it be Jake.

Chapter Fifteen

She gripped the gun tighter, careful to avoid the trigger. What would she do if it was Mossman? The servant shivered and watched her with huge eyes.

Her hands were literally shaking, and her sweaty finger went to the trigger when Jake appeared in the doorway.

"Mossman got away," he said. Fine beads of sweat glistened on his forehead, and he looked pale again. "Whoa, put that thing down before you shoot somebody. Namely me." He held up his hands in faux surrender. It was then she realized the gun had been actually pointing at him. She carefully set it down.

The servant shrieked and ran out of the room.

"Where'd he go?" she asked, wiping her sweaty hands off on her shirt.

Jake's expression turned sour. "He got away when I tripped over one of the damned hedges in his botanical garden of a backyard. That gave him the chance to get into his car and make a run for it."

She looked at the gun she'd laid on the mahogany desk. She'd been the one who'd distracted him and made him lose Mossman. "It's my fault you lost him. But I was worried when you went inside and didn't come out again."

"Let's not lay blame. Instead, let's get out of here before Mossman or his butler calls for backup." He waited for her to push away from the desk and join him. He squeezed her hand and pulled her toward the door before looking back at the gun on the desk. "Hold on a minute," he said. Letting go of her hand, he went back and wiped her prints off of the weapon.

For a moment, she thought he was going to take the gun with them.

"With everything else this man has tried, you don't need him to have your prints on a gun he can use against you." He also wiped off the edges of the desk. He took a moment in front of the computer before searching inside the desk drawers. He grabbed a card, and they headed out.

On their way across the front lawn toward their car, she saw the servant peeking out from the open front door. She mouthed the words, I'm sorry to him. She really didn't think the older fellow knew what Mossman was involved in. Or maybe she really was too naïve, even after everything that had happened to her. She glanced back again and hated that she'd just evolved from naïve to bitter.

"Where are we going? And can you slow down? I'm getting a cramp in my leg." She hobbled along in order to keep up.

Jake held up a business card. "Found this on the desk when I wiped the prints away. We're going to the InfoFero Company. Hurry. If my hunch is right, that's where Mossman is."

"What makes you think he'd go there?"

"I read part of an e-mail on his computer screen before we left. He'd started an e-mail telling someone the important papers were at his office."

"There's a good chance that's where he's going then," she said.

"With his hit man in jail, he's probably panicking because there's no doubt Cranston will talk his head off if he thinks it'll lessen his prison sentence."

He drove fast and they took the wrong street once. By the time they pulled up in front of InfoFero, the sun had set and the building was fully lit. Lights were on in every office. "Is it open?" Liz asked.

"I don't think so. Stay here."

"No way. You'd better let me come with you this time so I don't interrupt again."

He sighed. "I shouldn't let you do this."

"Like you have a choice," she said.

"Promise you'll stick with me?"

She nodded vigorously.

The front door was unlocked. That made her edgy. They stepped into the main lobby, where a guard sat at the desk eating a sandwich. He put the bread down. "May I help you?" he asked, wiping a crumb off his chin.

"We're here to see Vince Mossman."

He looked at both of them strangely. "We're closed."

"Yeah, but I know Mossman's here, and this is very important."

The security guard looked Jake over. "You're outta luck, mister."

"Look, I really need to see him." Jake whipped out his wallet and pulled out a couple of large bills. The guard's gaze shifted left to right, then he grabbed the bills.

"He's been here, but he left about ten minutes ago. I don't expect him back this week. He's on his way to Europe in his private jet."

"Can we catch him before he leaves?"

"Doubt it," the guard said. "The jetport is only two streets over, and the jet was already waiting for him. He's probably gone by now."

Jake leaned against the counter. "Great! What do we do now?"

Liz watched the guard blanch at the sight of bloodstains on Jake's sleeve. "Look, I can ask his partner if he can see you." He edged his hand toward the phone.

"Partner!" They looked at each other. Hope reappeared in Jake's eyes.

"Tell him that Jake Johnston has to see him, and it's urgent."

Liz pulled him gently aside. "It's one thing to ask about Mossman in the lobby, but going to his partner's office? I don't think we should," she said.

"Probably right."

She glanced at the guard, who was talking on the phone and watching them. He hung up.

"He wants to see you," the guard said.

"I'm sorry. We don't have time after all," she said quickly.

The elevator door dinged, and a man stepped out.

"Do you think the partner knows what's going on?" she whispered.

"I have the feeling we're about to find out."

There was something familiar about the wavy gray hair of the man talking to the guard. When he looked up and smiled at them, Liz gasped.

"Uncle Brody?"

"Liz?" He looked shocked. "Can it really be you? Darling, how'd you find me?" He opened his arms to her, and she ran to him, laughing and crying at the same time.

"I've been trying like mad to find you," Uncle Brody said, waving the security guard off.

Liz let her uncle go long enough to notice the new lines etched into his face since the last time she'd seen him.

"I've been so worried about you, honey. I'd only heard about John and Sarah after the house blew up. I couldn't believe it. I thought you were dead, too. I thought I'd lost you forever until the police told me it wasn't you in the building." His voice sounded thick and emotional, not something she'd ever seen before in her uncle. A tear escaped the corner of his eye.

Jake stepped up next to her. "Liz?"

She touched his good arm. "Jake, this is my Uncle Brody. Broderick Steinberg. The man I told you I'd been trying to find, but couldn't because I thought he was working in the Persian Gulf."

Uncle Brody cleared his throat and glanced at the security guard. "Let's take this conversation upstairs to my office, shall we?"

The elevator ride was quick. They stepped off directly onto the penthouse floor, and Brody's office was one of two on the floor. Once inside, she said, "I couldn't find your address after Mom and Dad died. I had no idea how to contact you." She glanced around the office. "What are you doing here?"

He appeared disconcerted at that. "We've got some talking to do, dear. But first, why is this young man with you?"

Liz watched the two men size each other up. Jake eyed Brody with distrust, while Uncle Brody assessed him right back.

It suddenly struck her that her uncle was the partner of the man who was trying to kill her. What did it mean? Uncle Brody still held her hand as if he never wanted to let go again. He loved her. She knew it. He couldn't be behind her attacks.

* * * * *

Jake looked at the slim, mustached man in his impeccable suit and wondered if he could be dangerous.

"What's your name, son?"

"Jake Johnston. I'm Liz's next-door neighbor in Fredericton." Instantly, he knew by the hurt in Liz's eyes that he'd made a mistake in introducing himself as a neighbor. It was true they'd become more than just neighbors, so why was he still denying it? "Liz and I have been trying to stay one step ahead of your partner, Vince Mossman. Are you aware he's been trying to kill your niece?"

Brody sucked in a hard breath. "What?"

"He very nearly succeeded a couple of times, too." Jake held up his bandaged arm as evidence.

"I don't understand. Why would Vince do that?" Brody's eyes narrowed, and his expression darkened. He made no move to let go of Liz. "Darling, are you sure it was Vince?"

Liz nodded. "We're very sure. Jake caught the hit man before he had a chance to hurt me. He's being held by the police in Toronto. It was the hit man who gave us enough information to find Mossman."

"I want to speak with this man," Brody said, but he made no move to leave Liz. "But first, I need to speak to Vince." He picked up the phone to dial an extension.

"Don't bother. He's taken off already," Jake said.

"Taken off? Where?" If Brody was acting, he was damned good at it.

"According to your security guard, he's gone somewhere on the company's private jet."

"He's not scheduled to go anywhere. What's going on?" Brody said.

"That's what we'd like to know," Liz said, looking at Jake then back at her uncle.

"What exactly happened to your arm?" Brody asked.

Jake slowly moved his arm and touched the dried blood with his hand. "Your partner's thug shot me while trying to kill Liz."

Brody looked stunned. "Who shot you?"

"Name's Bert. Lucky for us, he isn't a crack shot."

Brody obviously recognized the name Bert. "Why would Vince want to kill Liz?"

"We were hoping you could answer that question," Jake said. "But that was when we expected Mossman's partner to be a stranger, not Liz's uncle."

Jake stayed on guard while Broderick Steinberg crossed to the phone and buzzed the guard on the speakerphone.

"Collins," he barked. "Get Vince on the line!"

"I can't, sir," the guard said. "He left for Europe half an hour ago."

"What are you talking about? He's hosting a dinner party at his place tonight."

"I'm sorry, sir. I only know he asked me to call the jetport and book his flight plan and the pilot."

"Never mind. Thank you, Collins." Brody shut off the phone, and his expression softened when his gaze fell on Liz then focused on Jake. "Take a seat."

"I'll stand, thanks," he said.

"Suit yourself," Brody said.

"Uncle Brody, you haven't explained why you're here and not in the Persian Gulf," Liz said.

He sighed and looked down at his manicured fingernails. "I don't work in Saudi Arabia, Liz. I never did."

"I don't understand."

"Just a minute, honey. I have one more phone call to make first, then I'm going to explain everything to you. Prepare yourself for a bit of a shock."

He dialed and waited. "Bill, she's here. No, I haven't found that out yet. Just wanted you to know so you can stop worrying. Thanks a lot, Bill." He hung up.

"Bill? As in Bill Tait, my lawyer in Maine? How do you know him?"

"He's a friend of mine. I was in Europe all spring on business. It was a fairly complex venture, and I couldn't rely on junior staff to get it all straightened out." Brody sighed. "When I came home and found out that your...parents had been killed in a car accident and that your house had blown up after that, and you were probably dead, too, I was devastated."

"What does any of this have to do with Mossman?" Jake asked.

"To be frank, I'm not sure, but by God, we're going to find out what Vince is up to."

"Why couldn't I find your address, Uncle Brody? It was nowhere in the house."

He looked down at his hands and gripped them into fists. "I'll explain that, dear, but first I'd like to tell you what's been happening since you disappeared."

She nodded.

"When the police reported you didn't die in the explosion and you contacted Bill Tait, I couldn't believe my luck. I wanted to go to you right away, but Bill called and told me that you were on the road and he'd lost contact with you."

"Did you have people tailing us, too?" Jake asked between gritted teeth. He still didn't trust Steinberg.

"Of course not!"

"Maybe you should have collaborated with Mossman. He had Liz bugged and knew where she was most of the time."

"Now look here, young man, I am this girl's father, and I am here to tell you that the sun rises and sets on her as far as I'm concerned," he said angrily. Suddenly, he froze.

Liz frowned. "What did you say? You're my father?"

"I'm sorry, dear, but it's the truth."

"It can't be. Mom and Dad?"

He shook his head and sighed. "Good people. The best."

"Good people? They were my parents. Dad was your stepbrother."

"No, Liz. I'm sorry. They were very loyal but not related to me or to you." He tried to take her hand again, but she pulled it away. "I'm so sorry. This isn't the way I wanted to tell you."

* * * * *

"You're saying you're my father? My real father?" She could feel the blood rushing out of her face and heading straight for her toes. Everything started to go dark.

"Put her head between her knees," Brody barked at Jake and jumped up to get

water for her.

Jake gently pushed her head forward. She took several large breaths.

"I'm okay now." She sat back up slowly and leaned her head against the back of the leather sofa. The man who'd always been her uncle crouched on his knees now in front of her.

He held out a glass. "Take a sip," he said.

She sipped. "I'm not sure I can believe any of this, but if it is true, how could you do it? Why did you pretend to be my uncle all these years if you're really my father?"

"I need a little time to explain, dearest." He patted her hand, then got up off the Oriental rug and brushed off his pant legs. "I loved your mother more than life itself." He got a faraway look on his face. "I'm sorry to tell you this, but she died. She wasn't supposed to have a baby. She'd always had trouble with her blood pressure, and the doctors warned her against having a child. When she learned of her pregnancy, they wanted to do an abortion, but she wouldn't hear of it." He looked down at Liz lovingly, as if to tell her that he didn't blame her for her mother's death. "She wanted you so badly, nothing would stop her."

Brody crossed to the window and slid his fingers through the metal strips of the venetian blinds, making them clink while he looked out at the city beyond. "Before you were born, your mother began having serious complications due to her blood pressure." He pressed two fingers to the bridge of his nose. "In order to be able to explain your mother's reasons for the things she did, I have to tell you that she grew up in the US South, where her father, your grandfather…" Brody hesitated and looked back at Liz for a moment. "He was very wealthy and extremely unscrupulous. Your mother was a kind, loving woman. She was always fair and generous, but because of her father, she detested money and people who abused it. As soon as she was old enough, she ran away and got a job. She worked in the States until she could get a Canadian working visa and ended up in Toronto."

Brody's voice cracked. "We met and fell in love. I didn't tell her I was wealthy at first, because I was afraid she'd only want me for my money." He laughed wryly. "Little did I know she would have dropped me instantly had she known I was a successful businessman. She wanted nothing to do with wealth."

Liz listened intently.

"When I finally told her the truth, I thought I'd lost her for good, but by that time she loved me as much as I loved her. We had ten fabulous years together before you came along, and in that time, she began to learn that all wealthy people don't use their money for the wrong reasons. I believe she was truly happy, but her youth had scarred her deeply. There are some things even love can't fix." He grimaced. "What she asked of me was terrible, but I promised her on her deathbed, and I had to carry through." He turned and faced Liz. "You have brothers and a sister. I have three children from a previous marriage."

Liz couldn't believe her ears. The story kept getting more and more unbelievable.

He nodded. "I had custody of the children when your mother and I married. I'm afraid I overindulged them, and she saw three spoiled children who didn't appreciate life's simpler things, and she compared their lives with her own upbringing." He shrugged his shoulders. "Unfortunately, being a busy businessman, I had left a lot of their upbringing to the nanny. I'd failed my own children, so I had a lot to make up for."

"I can't believe this." Liz looked at Jake.

"Your mother made me promise not to let you grow up as a spoiled, rich child. She wanted you to live a simple existence and learn to appreciate life's gifts before becoming the daughter of a rich man."

He shook his head, and his eyes filled with tears. "Losing her was the worst day of my life, but your birth became a gift. The most beautiful gift your mother could give me. I'd lost the love of my life, but I had gained the most beautiful daughter. The minute I held you in my arms, my heart filled until I thought it might burst. At the same time, grief tore at me in more ways than one after her funeral, because before you were born, I'd promised your mother that if anything happened to her because of her illness, I would carry out her wishes for you. It was the only thing that gave her peace."

Liz got up and stood next to Jake. His arm went around her shoulders.

"Please understand that your mother was in a very fragile state. If I hadn't promised her, it could have killed her right then and there. I still had hope at that time that she might survive or she might change her mind. When I agreed to honor her wishes, we also agreed that I would tell you the truth when you were twenty-five. The only way I could keep my promise to her was to have my very good friends, John and Sarah, adopt you. They raised you as their own child. They loved you. And they kept me fully informed about you at all times. As often as I could, I came to visit, and it broke my heart every time I left you behind." He ran his hand across his eyes wearily. "Do you remember Christmases when you were very young with your brothers and sister?"

Frowning, she said, "I think I do!"

"We did that until you started asking why you weren't with your parents. Then we had to stop. Your brothers and sister are so excited to be with you again. They've been anxiously awaiting your twenty-fifth birthday this year as much as I have. They grew up to be pretty decent young adults, by the way, thanks to your mother's love and tender care. I only wish she could've been here to see it. And to see you."

Liz slowly walked toward her father. "It's all true, isn't it? I do remember those Christmases. I remember the other children. How could I have forgotten them?" She threw herself into his arms again and kissed his cheek. Tears poured down her face. "You must have loved my mother very much. But at the same time, I always knew how much you loved me, too, even if I did think you were my uncle."

"I'm so sorry, baby. The only thing that got me through the torment day-by-day was the realization that I could tell you the truth when you were twenty-five, and I prayed that you would forgive me for abandoning you." He broke down and cried openly.

She hugged him tightly as he sobbed into her shoulder. "Oh, Uncle Brody, I mean Dad. I've always adored you. Mother was very lucky to have found an honorable man like you. I love you very much!"

Jake crossed the room and put his arms around her, too, while her father reached over and hugged both of them. Later, he still sniffled and wiped at his eyes with a tissue he'd taken from his suit coat pocket. Every time he looked at her, he'd start to tear up again.

"I need some tissues," Liz said at last. Her shirt felt completely wet from her tears. Her father crossed to his desk and got the whole box of tissues.

She wiped at her face and reached out and handed one to Jake, too, who sheepishly gave a quick swipe of his nose.

Finally, they sat and faced each other around an oval coffee table.

"I guess my poor mother must have really had a horrible life to ask such a thing of you." It felt funny but wonderful at the same time to call him Dad. It hurt that she'd never meet her mother. "You couldn't have picked better adoptive parents for me, and you were always in my life, too. You never missed a birthday or a Christmas. You were at my graduation both from high school and university. How many children can say that of their father? You never missed one special occasion in my life, no matter where we lived at the time."

She looked down at her hands. "I had two fathers who never missed special times in my life." Her throat felt sore when she swallowed.

"We've got a lot of catching up to do, though, honey."

"I can't wait." Her face shone.

"We're forgetting one thing," Jake said. "I hate to bring it up at this time, but someone is trying to kill your daughter, Brody. Your partner."

"Tell me everything you know," Brody said.

Liz took a deep breath and started on that first day when her brakes had been cut and ended with taking Hugh through three provinces with them to find out what was going on.

Brody looked at his daughter with renewed pride and gratitude. "You're quite something, Liz. You've got guts!"

"And how." Jake laughed.

"I think you obviously have something to crow about, too, young man." Brody gave Jake a thankful look. "You've taken very good care of my daughter, including getting yourself shot in the bargain. I think there's more going on here than one neighbor helping another." He winked at Liz.

She smiled shyly at Jake, and he returned the smile.

"Now, as for Vince." Brody stood. "Come along, let's just see if we can find something in Vince's office to give us a clue as to why he would do this horrible thing. And to think I trusted that man."

Brody led them to the next office. He stepped inside and switched on the lights. The office furniture looked skewed, the desk barely visible with papers scattered all over it. His wall safe was open and empty. There was little doubt that he'd grabbed everything he could in a short time.

Uncle Brody sifted through the papers on the desk until he stopped and read a bit of one page. "I think I've found the reason." His expression turned angry. He held up several papers held together by a little blue triangle of paper.

"What is it?" Liz tried to look over his arm to see what the papers said.

"It's a copy of my last will and testament. How stupid could I have been? Vince was to become president and executor of my estate upon my death, but only if something happened to you. This business is willed to you, Liz. I was so proud that you got your degree in business—a chip off the old block. You're the only one of my children interested in business. The others all have their own assets and lives. They didn't want this." She noticed her father's hands shook slightly as he indicated the building.

"He probably planned on doing you in next, Brody," Jake added, trying to get a glimpse of the paperwork himself.

"I think you may be right, Jake. That bastard! I'm going to make that man pay. He's going to be in jail for a very long time, if I have anything to say about it."

"Except for the fact that he's now on his way to Europe," Liz said.

She hated to be the one to admit it, but Mossman was getting away.

Chapter Sixteen

Later that day in her father's boardroom, Liz watched while Brody laid out the paperwork he'd gathered from Vince's office. "I'm shocked that Vince managed to get so many of my personal papers. He even had my personal banking information," he said.

"How long have you two been partners?" Jake asked.

"Too long for this to have happened to me," Brody said, looking disgusted. He rifled through another stack of papers that had littered Mossman's office floor. "I trusted that man like a brother. I can't understand what drove him to do this. He's half-owner in the company, and he makes plenty of money."

"Maybe he got himself in debt," Jake said.

"What kind of debt would drive a man to murdering his best friend's daughter?"

"Depends on the man," Jake said.

Brody looked at Jake with renewed respect. He shook his head in agreement, but the truth weighted his shoulders. "Apparently, I've greatly misjudged him."

Liz listened. She still felt dazed by the latest bit of news about her uncle really being her father. She kept looking at him over and over again. She'd seen the resemblance, but he was supposed to be her uncle, so of course they looked alike. So much had happened in the past few months, from her parents dying, to her being targeted by a hit man… Learning that her uncle was actually her biological father seemed to be her tipping point.

Thank heavens Jake had come here with her. They might not have known each other long, but he had become her rock. She'd come to not only rely on him, but she'd fallen for him. Hard. She eyed him across the table from her.

Jake turned his chair sideways to talk to her father. It was then she noted the blood seeping through his shirt again. In her fog, she'd completely forgotten about him being shot.

"Jake, you're bleeding again. I think we should get you to a hospital," she said. "You probably need stitches."

He unbuttoned his shirt sleeve and rolled it up. Under the towel the wound had turned deep purple and looked nasty. She hissed through her teeth. "It looks worse."

"Maybe because Mossman dug his nails into it."

Brody looked at Jake's arm. "If that viper scratched you with his nails, you'll be needing a tetanus shot as well, I'd wager."

Within minutes they were on their way in her father's chauffeur-driven car.

Thankfully, since Mossman would be taken out of the will very shortly, the man would have no reason to try to kill her, no matter what country he escaped to. Hugh would go to jail, and he'd give up whatever information he had about Mossman in the process.

An hour later, she and Brody were still waiting for Jake in the waiting room. Short of pacing back and forth, she couldn't wait a minute longer to find out how he was doing. She jumped nervously to her feet. "I'll be right back, Unc...Dad."

Her father grinned. "Take your time, sweetheart. I'll be here waiting."

Liz crossed to the nurse's station. "May I go inside and check on Jake Johnston?"

"Sure, he's in room one-twelve." The nurse gave her a wry look. "He could probably use some company." She looked at Liz carefully then lowered her voice. "Due to the nature of his injury, he'll have to wait for the police to arrive before he can leave. It could be awhile."

"Thanks." She shuddered at what that poor man had endured for her. She twisted back to her father. "Want to come in with me...Dad?" Happiness lit his face every time she called him Dad, but she still fought the urge to call him uncle. Maybe because she'd loved her adoptive father and mother beyond words. Nothing could change that, but she loved this man, too. Knowing that he was her real father made it that much easier.

"No, honey. I'll wait here. You go ahead."

She saw Jake lying on a bed before he saw her. His arm had been stitched but not bandaged yet. She guessed it was left uncovered for the police's benefit.

"Hey. How are you feeling?" she asked.

He opened his eyes slowly. "I'm doing well. In fact, I'm almost as tough as you," he said. "Although I might have complained a bit more than you ever did, especially after all those horrific accidents Hugh caused." Jake's brow furrowed. "Liz, I'm so sorry I didn't believe you."

She bit her lip and sank into the chair next to his bed. "I wasn't even sure I believed myself. Hugh did a good job of making me look crazy." She forced a weak grin. "But even though you weren't sure about me, you still stayed around and protected me. Most men wouldn't have done that. I'm very grateful."

A voice outside the door halted their conversation. An officer stepped inside, and for the next half hour, they spent their time making a report.

Finally bandaged and with a fresh tetanus shot, Jake led the way to the waiting room. Her father jumped to his feet and smiled. He'd been talking on his phone, but he'd hung up quickly at the sight of the couple.

Liz fought back the sensation that something had ended. Maybe because Jake no longer needed to protect her. And most likely he had to get back to his life, his job. He was free of her. Her heart tugged harder, and she suddenly felt like crying again.

* * * * *

Back at her father's place, he said, "Jake, maybe you should get some rest?"

Liz noted his pallor. He probably did need rest. He'd been going with the untreated bullet wound for a whole day before he'd had it stitched.

Jake nodded. "I think I'll take you up on that, Brody."

Liz followed him to the bottom of the stairs with every intention of making sure he got upstairs without feeling weak. He stopped her with a hand on her shoulder. "I'll make it on my own. Take some time to get reacquainted with your dad."

She felt torn. She needed time with Uncle...her father. But she also wanted to talk to Jake. She hadn't talked to him about the situation since everything had hit the fan in her father's office. "But..."

"Go," he said. "Be with your father. I'll see you later." Their eyes met, and she wanted to tell him how she felt about him. Was it the right time? Maybe he just wanted to go home and forget this episode had ever happened. After all, she came with a lot of baggage.

Jake didn't give her a chance to make up her mind. He started climbing the stairs to the room he'd been given without looking back.

Brody waited in the den, a large room with chandeliers and a stone fireplace. Fabergé eggs sat on a black marble display piece. The room glistened, and somewhere in the recesses of her foggy memory, she remembered a Christmas tree in this room. Decorated with homemade ornaments rather than expensive decorations that matched the room. There'd been a lot of laughter and hugs and love here.

She and her father talked for hours, and finally she looked at her watch. "I should check on Jake," she said. Her father looked a little worn out, too. It had been a tiring day for everyone.

Brody kissed her forehead. "Go after him, sweetie," he said.

She knocked lightly on the door, which was already ajar. "Jake? You awake?" Jake was on the bed with his good arm draped across his eyes when she entered the room.

"Yes," he said.

"Are you still in pain?" She winced at his heavily bandaged arm. Seeing it at the hospital, she'd realized his injury had been deeper than she'd first believed.

He lifted the arm that had been shielding his eyes. "No, they gave me something for pain. I think I'm covered." He shifted up on his good arm and smiled at her. "Actually, I'm feeling no pain at all."

She shook her head. "I'm so sorry to have put you through all of this." She perched on the edge of his bed. Her father had put him into another room she actually remembered. It must've belonged to one of the boys, because the décor remained unchanged. There were still posters on the walls and ball gloves and bats in the room.

She wrung her hands. "How can I thank you enough for everything you've done for me?" She pressed her lips together to offset the lump growing in her throat. "You're a true hero."

"Yeah, right. I might have been more of a hero if I'd believed you to start with."

"Don't think that way. No one could have figured out what was going on without help. It was too convoluted, and I was missing crucial information, like the fact that Brody is my father and not my missing uncle."

"I should have known you weren't unhinged, though." He looked so guilty she had to laugh.

"Unhinged? Well, now, that's a lovely thing to say." She laughed. "Jake. Give yourself permission to accept praise. You're a very good friend. You helped me when no one else would even believe me. Even though you didn't quite trust your instincts at first, they were dead right."

"Thanks. I appreciate that." He dropped back down against the pillow. "So what's next?"

"Pardon?"

"What'll you do now that you can put your life back in order?"

She smiled at him. "Uncle Brody...Dad—it still feels strange to say that—wants me to stay here. I think I have to come to terms with everything first. I need to go home, get everything in order and then I'll decide from there."

"Uh," he said stiffly. "That makes sense."

He didn't touch her. He didn't try to kiss her. She badly wanted him to. "We'll talk later?" she said finally, noticing that he really did look pale.

"Later," he said.

It was into the wee hours of the morning when the two detectives they'd met at the police station came to the house. Liz and Brody talked to them first before they quizzed Jake in his room.

Everyone slept in the next day and when Jake came down for breakfast, he didn't eat much and went back to bed before she had a chance to talk to him alone again.

Last night she'd slept in the room that had been hers since she was born. Or so her dad told her. It was pristine. A beautiful daughter's room, but it felt brand new and never lived in. She'd crawled into bed and cry for her parents. Cry for herself, her loss and her loneliness since her adoptive parents' deaths. And she'd wanted to cry for missing out on her biological family. But in the end, she really understood why her mother took the steps she had to protect her daughter. Liz had survived everything, probably because she'd never been pampered. She'd learned to be self-sufficient. And now she needed to sleep for a week.

The police turned up again the next day while they were having lunch.

"I'm here because I've got good news. Due to a repair issue with your company's private plane, we managed to apprehend Vince Mossman and Bert Johnson at the Sarnia Chris Hadfield airport yesterday. They are both currently in custody."

Liz reached over and squeezed Jake's hand on top of the table.

"Should we come down to the precinct right now?" her father asked, jumping up from the table and throwing his napkin down.

The officer held up a hand. "No. We'll contact you when we have everything in order. The captain just wanted you to know we're on top of the situation."

"I'm grateful," Brody said. "Thank you for the great news."

When the officer left, they all stared at each other for a few moments until everyone started talking at once.

When the excited chatter died down, Brody said, "I want to talk to Vince face-to-face. I trusted that bastard. We were best friends, partners. There has to be a reason he'd do this. Not just because he was greedy. I know him." Her father paused. "At least I thought I knew him. Not that I'll ever forgive him for trying to kill my daughter."

"Luckily, your daughter managed to thwart him at every turn," Jake said, smiling at her.

"It didn't exactly feel like I was being successful, but I guess I managed to stay alive throughout the whole thing, if that's what you call thwarting."

"Most people would have panicked. They wouldn't have had the presence of mind to protect themselves the way you did, Liz. You have shown yourself to be a very strong young woman," her father added.

She shrugged and took a drink of her coffee, brushing off their comments. They had no idea how afraid she'd been. She didn't feel brave at all.

The rest of the meal was much lighter. Her father looked much more relieved when they moved to the living room, where they sat and chatted.

Before long, Jake left Liz alone with her dad again. He was very considerate.

Brody patted the couch. "Come sit beside me, darling," he said. "Did you sleep last night?"

"Very well. I was exhausted."

He frowned and considered his fingernails for a moment. "Listen, do you want me to call a counselor? No matter how well you managed, you've been through a lot, and I have a friend who would happily sit down with you."

She considered his statement and understood why he'd made the suggestion. "I appreciate it, Dad, but I honestly don't think I need it. I think I'll sleep better at night knowing I can look after myself."

He grinned. "Yeah, you're my kid, all right."

She laughed. "I'm guessing my stubborn streak is genetic?"

He nodded. "Actually, when you're ready, you and I have some serious talking to do. Besides wanting you to come back here and to get to know your family, I'm in need of a partner. One with a business degree, preferably. What do you say?"

"Dad, there's nothing I'd like better."

He looked serious. "But?"

"But there are a few things I have to figure out first. Can you give me time to do that?"

He nodded in acknowledgment and patted her hand. He didn't smile, but his eyes sparkled lovingly at her. "Of course. Take whatever time you need. Just stay safe and be sure to come back to us as soon as possible."

She treasured the way she could see herself in this man she'd adored her whole life. She hadn't realized that such a thing could be important to her. At the same time, she felt a pang for the parents who'd raised her. She missed them terribly. She really wished they could have been here with her right now, enjoying this moment.

"And maybe you have a certain someone you've got to talk a few things over with?" he asked, smiling.

She picked at her jeans. "I guess." She really wasn't sure what Jake would say. How would he react if she walked up to him and said, Hey, I love you, mister. Do you love me, too?

There was still that neighbor-helping-neighbor comment he'd made to her father that bothered her. Since he'd saved her, maybe he'd resolved his personal issues and could move on?

Maybe that meant he'd leave and go back to his life—without her. No sense denying it. She'd fallen for him and couldn't bear the thought of losing him, but she was afraid he didn't feel the same way.

By the time she got upstairs, she knocked lightly on his door. He was sound asleep, so she went to her bedroom. Sleep didn't come easily that night. So many things were going through her head. Finally, at around eight in the morning she got up and went downstairs. Her father must be an early bird, since he was already having coffee and reading the paper.

"Morning, dear." He stood and pulled her into his arms and hugged her.

"Is Jake still asleep?" she asked, hugging him back and grabbing a coffee cup from the sideboard. She'd decided last night to lay it all out. Tell him that she loved him.

Her father frowned. "I thought you knew. Jake left early this morning."

Liz's face fell. "He left? Just like that?"

"Honey, I tried to get him to stay, but he said you've got a lot of catching up to do with your newfound family. He told me to tell you that he wishes you good luck."

"Good luck?" Heat built at the backs of her eyes, and she blinked rapidly to dispel the tears. She got to her feet and went to the window to look out at the backyard.

"It's not as bad as all that," her father said. "I have the feeling he cares about you very deeply and that's why he's giving you space right now. I could tell the poor guy was actually agonizing over leaving you alone with your loving family." He laughed. "I felt bad for him. To be honest, I assumed you two had talked and agreed this was for the best."

"No. Maybe he doesn't care about me. He's helped me, and it's over." Her voice hitched, and she wouldn't meet her father's gaze.

"So what's your next move?" her father asked.

She looked at him seriously. "I guess it'll be reuniting with my siblings. I can't believe I have brothers and a sister. Do you think they'll accept me?"

Her father grinned. "They can't wait to see you. They've been as worried about you as I have." His expression grew serious. "But that's not what I meant, Liz. I meant what are you going to do about Jake?"

"I'm not sure what you mean. He left without even saying good-bye. I think that says it all."

"You love him. And I saw the way he looked at you, darling… He feels the same way."

Her heart started pounding in her chest. "Really? Do you really think he loves me?"

Her father laughed. "I'm positive."

"Then why'd he leave me?"

"Because he loves you. He wants you to have time to come to terms with everything, I imagine."

She inhaled and bit back the excitement bubbling up. Could it be true?

He patted her hand. "Don't worry, it's all going to work out."

Chapter Seventeen

Three days later and due to a delay at the Toronto airport, her plane landed in Fredericton later than expected. It was almost midnight.

She looked at the borrowed Gucci suitcase beside her on the rear seat of the taxi and wondered if she should go straight to the hotel room and wait until morning. What if her father had been wrong about Jake's feelings? No. She had to see Jake, now. She felt as jittery as if she'd had ten cups of coffee.

The last few days with her family had been wonderful, except when she had had to go to the police station to make a statement. She'd been so happy to meet her siblings. They were wonderful people, all of them, and they'd formed an instant familial bond. And they had children. She had nieces and nephews. She couldn't wait to get to know them.

She knew it would have been the happiest moment of her life if only Jake had been there to share it with her.

Now here she was, taking a risk that she'd never believed possible of herself. She was going to his house to ask him if he loved her as much as she loved him.

She exited the taxi, cringing when she saw the house she'd been renting. Her exploding car had obviously done quite a job on the plastic siding. It looked like a cake with blobbed icing dripping off the sides.

She made a mental note to contact the poor landlord and compensate him once she got back on her feet. She sighed, if he didn't already have a lawsuit pending.

She reached for Jake's doorbell. Thankfully, his lights were still on. There was a chill in the air tonight.

A cool breeze felt like it spun around her several times as she waited and listened for his footsteps. Goose bumps raised on her arms.

Her heart rate quickened at the sound of approaching footsteps. What if he wasn't happy to see her? What if her father had been wrong about him and Jake had been glad to see the last of her?

Suddenly unsure of his reaction to her showing up unannounced, she considered coming back in the morning.

He flicked on the outside light. "Liz!"

It surprised her to see Jake in the doorway with his jacket on and a suitcase in one hand. He dropped it and immediately pulled her into his arms. "What are you doing here? I've missed you." He held her close and kissed her hair, sending thrills of electricity through her.

"Sorry to show up unannounced. I thought we needed to talk. I booked a hotel, but I had to come here first." She waited breathlessly for his reaction. He took her case and set it beside his.

She suddenly felt awkward. "Why did you leave without telling me, Jake?"

"I thought you needed some time with your family." He shrugged. "Besides, I had some thinking to do of my own."

"Don't tell me you had thinking to do because you thought you let me down or something foolish like that. You saved my life—twice!"

"Twice?" He appeared perplexed.

"The first time when you called me to your place. I would have been blown up in the car."

Eyebrows raised, he nodded slowly, light dawning in his eyes. "Does that negate the time I let you be abducted and nearly killed?"

"You didn't exactly have a choice in the matter." She reached up and touched his arm. "How's it feeling?"

"Fine." He stiffened at her touch. Had she read everything the wrong way, after all?

"And your head?"

"Brain damage was minimal." He grinned.

She laughed but it sounded forced.

She decided to throw it all out there. "Why did you really leave me in Ontario without telling me you were going?"

"For one very important reason." He looked down at his hands, cleared his throat, then looked at her again. "Because I love you, and I needed to consider a few things before I declared my intentions."

Her heart started to thud like a piston working overtime. "You do? Is that why you have a suitcase?"

He nodded but didn't move from his spot. "I was flying back to Ontario."

She could feel the heat of his body, so close, so tempting. "You were coming back for me?"

"I was. And I had a really good scenario lined up...very romantic." He pulled her against him and nibbled at her earlobe.

"I thought you were trying to be chivalrous and trying to help me because you wanted to prove something to yourself." Her mouth turned up at the corners weakly, with no hint of a smile. "After everything you've thought about me and the way I..."—she looked away—"put your life at risk. How can you care for me? I've been nothing but trouble since the first day you met me."

"Don't forget you saved my life when I had a pistol pointed at my head. If it wasn't for your ingenuity and bravery, who knows what might have happened? And I kind of enjoyed the show, myself." He winked at her.

A slow flush crept up her neck and face.

"What haunts me is the fact that I didn't believe you in the beginning. I promised to keep you safe then let that bastard take you away without breaking a sweat. I have a lot to make up to you."

"No one else would have helped me. They would have just thought I was crazy." Her eyes burned. "Just wait until you meet my brothers and sister. In some ways, we're very much alike."

His eyebrows lifted mischievously. "I hope not the getting-in-trouble part."

"Funny man." She tipped her face up to him. "Aren't you going to kiss me?"

His eyes darkened, yet he hesitated. "If I do, there's no turning back. Because every time I touch you, it's like an electric charge that drives me wild," he warned.

She smiled at him. "It's like that for me, too. Nuclear fusion! I'll say it again. Aren't you going to kiss me?" She gave him the sexiest, most wanton smile that she knew how to give.

Their lips met.

"Before we get carried away, I have a question. Will you marry me?" he asked.

"I will." She smiled at him. "And just think, when we move in together, I won't even have much to pack. I don't own a thing."

"Why would you want to pack? I'm the one who's moving."

"You are?"

"I've always wanted a job as a climatologist in Ontario. Now's my chance." He started unbuttoning his shirt and luring her deeper into his house.

"But your job here…"

"You've got a lifetime of catching up to do with your family. I want to be there with you and help you enjoy every minute of it."

She watched him undo the last button and pull his shirt out of his jeans. She grinned. "Am I going to have to teach you to swivel your hips when you do that?"

His initial shocked reaction quickly turned to fire. "I think you are!"

She fell into his arms, and he covered her with kisses.

~End~

Message from the Author

Thank you for investing that most precious of commodities—your time—in my book! If you enjoyed UNKNOWN ASSAILANT, I would be thrilled if you could help us buzz it. You can do this by:

Recommending it. Help other readers find this book by recommending it to friends, readers' groups and discussion boards.

Reviewing it. Please share with other readers what you liked about this book by reviewing it wherever you purchased it, or at readers' sites such as Goodreads.

Again, thank you for choosing to read my book!

If you don't want to miss my next release, you can sign up for Lina's newsletter here: NEWSLETTER. A bonus to signing up? Pop-up Giveaways which are open only to newsletter subscribers. Subscription to newsletter is also available on my Facebook page, Lina Gardiner Author.

Other books by Lina Gardiner:

Jess Vandermire Vampire Hunter Series
Grave Illusions (Book 1)
Beyond the Grave (Book 2)
Grave New Day (Book 3)
Grave Expectations (Book 4)
— coming in March 2015
~

Gift of Prophecy 2014
~

The Black Moon Series
Black Moon Awakening (Book 1)
~

What She Doesn't Know (Romantic Suspense)

About the Author

Lina Gardiner lives in New Brunswick, Canada. She is a Daphne DuMaurier and Prism Award winner in Dark Fantasy and has garnered a fabulous Kirkus review for Romantic Suspense. Her previous publications include romantic suspense and paranormal romance novels targeted to the adult market. She loves to hear from readers! Learn more about them on her website.

Connect with the Author:
Email: Lina Gardiner
Website: linagardiner.com
Blog: http://www.linagardiner.blogspot.ca
Twitter: https://twitter.com/LinaGardiner